Birthday Wishes

A HOLIDAY ROMANCE NOVELLA

DANIELLE BAKER

ISBN # 979-8-9880456-7-0

Formatting: Books From Beyond

Foreword

This is for all the girls that have
loved more than one book boyfriend at a time.
I couldn't choose, so you don't have to, either.

You can have your cake and eat it, too.
You're welcome, besties.

Please review Content and Trigger Warnings.
Your mental health matters.
Love you, book besties.

<u>Content/Trigger Warning:</u>

MFM Romance/Why Choose
Dub-Con/Edging/Bondage/Impact Play/Double Penetration
Mentions of Cancer in Remission (not on page)
Mentions of Fertility Issues
Sexual Harassment
Bigotry & Verbal Assault

Chapter One

"Is this seat taken?"

Hope Mackenzie raised her eyes from the skewer of olives she was pushing around in the dirty martini that sat in front of her. Giving the guy a halfhearted smile, she shook her head. He flashed her a grin before lowering his frame into the seat directly to her right.

He was moderately attractive, in a *his-wife-picks-out-his-clothes* or a *probably-lives-in-his-momma's-basement*, sort of way.

Her shoulders sagged dejectedly. Not that she had any room to talk. She'd probably be living in *her* momma's basement again in another few weeks, if she couldn't find a new apartment.

She resumed idly playing with the olives in her glass as he ordered a beer. The fancy hotel bar was bustling, but surprisingly not crowded for a Friday evening in the heart of Chicago. The lighting was dim, intimate. Glancing up and down the polished bar, she noticed several other empty seats on either side of her. He pivoted in his seat, angling his body toward hers. She sighed and braced herself, glancing down at his hand that was loosely clasped around the frosted draft beer glass. She rolled her eyes. Of course.

"I'm in town for a marketing seminar," the guy said conversationally, bringing his beer to his mouth. She didn't respond, not even pretending to listen. "Dirty martini, huh?"

She nodded once. Scanning the room around her, she watched as a man with dark, silver-streaked hair took a seat at the far end of the L shaped bar. The bartender made his way over to the newcomer. Moments later a highball glass with several inches of bourbon was passed across the bar to him. His long, wide fingers wrapped around the crystal glass and raised it to his lips. A thick, dark beard covered the lower portion of his face and jaw, and dark, penetrating eyes met hers as he took a drink of the bourbon. The man was a beast. Thick and barrel chested, his arms looked to be the size of her thighs... and her thighs were anything but small. Muscles rippled beneath the dark button-down shirt he wore, straining against the material. *Holy shit.* Something fluttered in her belly.

"Is that the only thing you like dirty?" the man next to her asked, bringing her attention back to him, and she raised her eyebrows in surprise at his forwardness.

"Do you routinely attempt to pick up random women at hotel bars?" she asked, raising her eyes to his, her voice flat. She nodded to his left hand, indicating the indent on his third finger that she had noticed earlier. Stupid fucker. "Does your wife know you're a cheating snake?"

His fingers flexed where they sat on the bar then curled into a fist. It's possible she read it wrong, and the reason he didn't have the ring on was the same reason her own engagement ring wasn't decorating her finger any longer. When she raised her eyes to his again, they flashed with annoyance, and she raised an eyebrow. No, her first guess was definitely correct, which he confirmed. "What she doesn't know won't hurt her."

She scoffed and turned to face forward again, picking up her martini. "Get lost, Skippy."

"You—"

"Hey, baby girl," a deep, husky voice murmured from behind her, a second before a hand drifted over the nape of her neck, making her shiver. "Sorry I'm late."

Hope raised her eyes and was struck speechless when she recognized the man from the other end of the bar. He was so much bigger up close. Like a tank. Or a bear. Or a bear riding a tank.

His dark, coffee brown eyes crinkled at the corners as he bestowed a knowing smile on her. Butterflies exploded in her belly, and the fingers at the nape of her neck strummed lightly. Then, those brown eyes shifted from hers to the man on the other side of her, and the coolness that filled them made her shiver again.

"This guy bothering you, baby girl?" he asked roughly, leaning his other elbow on the surface of the bar. The heady, citrus and cedarwood scent of him filled her senses. A dark, navy-blue shirt was buttoned down his broad chest. The top two buttons had been left undone, revealing several inches of tanned throat and chest. Crinkly, salt and pepper chest hair was visible in the opening, and she vaguely wondered if it was as soft as it looked. She blinked rapidly to dispel the intrusive thought.

Holy shit he's hot, she thought dazedly as she raised her eyes to his again.

"I was just sending him home to his wife," she murmured, and the breathiness of her voice made her blush to the roots of her blonde hair. "Isn't that right, Skippy?"

The other man rolled his eyes and stood from the chair, the legs scraping noisily on the polished floor. "Bitch," he muttered as he made to walk away.

"You wanna try that again?" another deep voice said, and Hope turned in her seat to see a tall blonde man stopped directly in front of Skippy. "You will apologize to our lady."

"Yours?" Skippy asked, shock making his voice come out higher, his eyes bouncing from one man to the other, to hers, and then back again. "Both of you?"

Hope's heart thudded in her chest, her breaths coming out

choppy. She swallowed hard. The blonde's eyes left Skippy's and found hers, a deep, emerald green the likes she'd never seen before. He had a clean-shaven face and a jawline that she wanted to run her fingers over. He wore a starched white, button-down shirt with the sleeves rolled to his elbows. Tattoos peeked out along his forearms. Black slacks fit his long legs.

Double holy shit.

"Mmmm," the blonde only murmured, before returning his gaze to Skippy. "Apologize to the lady. Now."

Skippy scoffed low in his throat and made to walk away but was brought up short when Blonde Henry Cavill gripped his elbow.

"Jesus. Sorry, lady," Skippy muttered sourly, yanking his arm out of the blonde Vikings hands. He walked away, leaving her with two of the hottest men she'd ever seen. Tall-Dark-and-Broody's fingers were still strumming along the nape of her neck as Mr. Steal-Your-Girl stepped forward into the space Skippy had vacated. The bartender stopped in front of them, asking for Blondies drink order, and he leaned in close to accept the drink that the bartender passed him a moment later. The smell of olive oil and lemon drifted off of him. He smelled good enough to eat.

A strange mix of fear and excitement skittered along her nerves. She knew enough to be wary of them... but she felt oddly safe with them, too. Heat spread along every nerve, skittering across her skin like tiny currents. She felt more alive than she had in a long time.

This is how women go missing, Hope, she thought to herself, glancing up at them both again.

Tall-Dark-and-Bearded finally pulled his hand away from the nape of her neck and flashed her a smile. "Sorry. I hope we didn't ruin your evening."

"No, thank you for rescuing me," she murmured, her voice still coming out all trembly. Damn they were hot. Outrageously, panty-meltingly hot.

"What brings you to Chicago?" he asked after taking a sip of his bourbon. His voice was impossibly deep, and the way it rumbled out of him made her already trembling fingers shake even more.

"I'm supposed to meet my sister here," she lied. If these men were trying to kidnap her, she wanted to make it seem like she wasn't here completely alone.

Tall-Dark-and-Handsome's dark brows pulled over his eyes in a frown and his lips thinned beneath the dark beard. "Have we scared you, baby girl?"

"No," she whispered, another half-lie. They made her nervous, sure. But scared? No. Intrigued? *Absolutely*.

"So, what brings you to the Windy City, really?" he asked, leaning his hip against the bar as he stood next to her. Blonde God to her right lowered himself into the seat vacated by Skippy, angling his body toward her. "And I will know if you lie to me again, baby girl."

She swallowed hard. This was... dangerous. And thrilling.

"I'm in town for my birthday," Hope murmured quietly, opting for honesty. Lowering her eyes to her drink, she stirred the olives around again. "It was supposed to be a weekend away with my fiancé, but..." she trailed off, the hurt lancing through her chest, then replaced with bubbling anger. She shook her blonde hair away from her face and straightened her shoulders. "Anyway. The hotel was non-refundable."

"So, you're here for a romantic birthday weekend and no man to spend it with?" Blonde God asked from her right, and she turned, nodding slowly as she was captivated by those green eyes fringed with long blonde lashes. "That's a damn shame."

The bourbon glass was set down on the bar as a large, strong looking hand was extended toward her. She looked up and placed her hand in his, and he raised it to his lips. His beard tickled the knuckles of her hand as he kissed it, butterflies taking flight in her

5

midsection at the sensation. "I'm Grant. This is my business partner, Van."

"So, a business trip?" she asked, settling back into her seat, glancing between the two men.

Grant nodded. "We own and operate a small restaurant together. I run the business side; Van is our executive chef. We're here for a food expo."

"Ahhh," she murmured, nodding. She turned toward the one named Van. "That's why you smell like olive oil and lemons."

Van laughed, showing her a captivatingly white smile. "Hazard of the trade."

"Well, it's very nice to meet you both. I'm Hope," she said quietly, shaking Grant's hand and then turning to shake Van's. His hands were scarred but deceptively soft to the touch. "And thank you again for rescuing me."

Grant motioned for the bartender, then said gruffly, "I'll take another bourbon, and please send out a dessert. It's her birthday."

"Yes, sir," the bartender said and disappeared, returning a moment later with the bourbon for Grant.

Hope protested, but several minutes later an oversized, gourmet chocolate cupcake was being placed in front of her, a single candle stuck in the ganache frosting. The flame flickered and bounced in the dim light.

Grant leaned down and pressed his lips close to her ear and whispered huskily, "I want you to make a wish, butterfly. Anything you want."

She shivered at the feel of his warm breath on her, the butterflies wreaking havoc on her insides again. Glancing up at him from beneath her lashes, she stared at him for a long moment before turning her head toward Van. He remained seated to her right, his elbow resting on the back of the chair and his long, slender fingers hovering near his mouth. His green eyes blazed into hers.

"Anything I want?" she asked on a whisper. *What was she doing?*

She wasn't this person... this woman that flirted shamelessly with not one, but two insanely hot strangers... But then Van raised his eyes to Grant's, where she could feel him standing to her left. She turned and raised her eyes to Grant's stupidly handsome face again, and he nodded slowly. *She could be that person... just for tonight, right? One little, totally insane birthday wish? She deserved a little fun after being a firsthand witness to her own life imploding this week, didn't she?*

Leaning forward, she pursed her lips and blew out the solitary candle, the wisp of smoke fluttering out of existence after the flame was extinguished. Three forks were stacked on the plate. Picking them up, she extended one each to Grant and Van. They each took one of the forks, Grant's looking tiny in his massive hand as Hope sliced into the cupcake.

It was the most intimate thing she'd done in a long time. Sharing a dessert. With two ridiculously hot strangers.

When the bartender had cleared away the empty plate, she smiled over at both of them shyly. "Thank you. That was divine, and totally unnecessary."

Grant leaned forward and raised his hand, and she froze as his thumb trailed over the corner of her mouth, picking up a smudge of chocolate. She blushed a million shades of crimson when he then brought his thumb to his own mouth, cleaning the pad of his thumb with his tongue. She damn near moaned at the eroticism of the act. Her entire body was on fire, tingling like a live wire had been touched to her skin.

"So, tell us little one, what's your wish?" Van asked from her right, his voice low and husky.

She bit her lip and raised her eyes to his, and then Grant's again, her breathing choppy. "I don't... I don't want to say it." She shivered again when Grant's hand returned to the nape of her neck, his thumb stroking the underside of her jaw as she looked up at him.

"Tell me," he growled, the rough rumble of his voice sending

7

jolts of electricity down her spine. "Say the words, Hope. What was your wish?"

She was trembling like a leaf. She bit her lip again and watched as Grant's dark eyes zeroed in on the movement. His eyes darkened and heat spread through her.

"I don't want to choose," she finally whispered, her voice shaking.

Chapter Two

"Say the words and you don't have to, baby girl," she heard Grant say, his voice so low and thick it made her squeeze her thighs tightly together, anything to alleviate the ache between them. *There's no way this is real life, right? Was she really going to do this?*

She glanced back at Van, who remained as he was, his fingers still loosely draped over his mouth as he stared at her, his dark green eyes intense. He nodded, too.

"Say the words, baby girl. We need to know this is what you want," Grant growled close to her ear again. A breathy moan slipped out of her lips before she could stop it. "But know that once you say those words, you're ours."

She nodded, taking a shuddering breath in. "Yes."

"Say it," Grant growled, his teeth clenched tightly. His fingers tightened on the nape of her neck, making her arch her neck slightly. "Now, Hope."

"I want you both," she breathed, her lips inches away from his at this point. "That's my wish."

Van stood then, his front pressed close against her right side, though he didn't touch her. "You want to be shared, little one?"

His breath ghosted over the side of her face, and she nodded. "You want us to fuck you at the same time?"

Holy shit, hearing him say the words... "Yes, please," she breathed, heat rushing to her cheeks. She glanced around the bar nervously.

"Have you been shared before, butterfly?" Grant asked from her left.

"No," she whispered, shaking her head. "Do you... do you do this often?"

Grant's fingers squeezed the back of her neck lightly. "A few times."

"Are you two a couple?" Hope asked then, her brows pulling together, her voice rising slightly.

Van chuckled, and the sound of it was smooth as melting butter. "No, little one. We're not in a relationship, and we don't cross swords. We just like to share from time to time."

"Do you want to get out of here, Hope?" Grant asked then, his fingers flexing on the back of her neck.

"Yes," Hope said without hesitation.

"Good girl," Grant murmured so low she could barely hear him, and she damn near melted into a puddle in her seat. He extended his hand to her, and she stood on trembling legs. Her dress had ridden up on her thighs and she tugged it down.

"Jesus, I knew you were stunning, but this dress..."

Hope blushed to the roots of her blonde hair. It had been a splurge for her birthday, a skintight bodycon dress that highlighted the narrowness of her waist and the full curves of her breasts and wide hips. The deep amethyst purple complimented her pale skin, blonde hair, and China blue eyes. The neckline cut diagonally across her chest, from the top of one shoulder to below her arm on the opposite side, leaving one arm completely bare.

She knew her size eighteen figure was soft and round. She had a big ass and thick thighs that were besties, a fact that Tony had never failed to remind her of in his clueless sort of way... but the way these two men were staring at her, as if she was the most beautiful thing they'd ever seen, with heat and lust in their eyes... she exalted in it. Tony had never looked at her like that, but she understood now *why*... Shoving the thoughts away, she stared up at them both, reveling in this moment of being desired and wanted.

Grant's hand came up and his fingers gripped her chin, tilting her face toward his. "Fuck, I'm going to tear this dress off of you with my teeth," Grant whispered darkly, and she clenched her thighs tightly together as wet heat pooled there at the filthy words. "Tonight, we're going to make you come with our tongues, our fingers, and our cocks, baby girl. Are you ready for that?"

Oh God. "Yes."

"Good, let's go."

Chapter Three

Grant paid for the drinks—hers included, of course, such a gentleman—then the three of them made their way through the hotel bar to the lobby toward the bank of elevators. Pressing the button, they waited for just moments before the doors slid open. Van had taken her hand in his as they walked, the warmth of his fingers wrapped around hers sending sparks up her arm and straight into her middle. Using her hand, he directed her into the elevator before them. The doors closed behind them and Hope gasped when Grant's hand closed around her throat. His fingers pressed on one side of her jaw while his thumb dug in on the other, tilting her face up toward his as he lowered his mouth to hers in a searing, open mouthed kiss. *Oh fuck. Yes.*

Her fingers tightened around Van's, still clasped together, and then she felt him step behind her, pressing his front to her back.

"Fuck you smell so good, little one," Van groaned from behind her, his other hand sinking into her hair at the back of her head, tugging back lightly, arching her neck and pushing her mouth more firmly against Grant's. Grant was thickly built with a set of impossibly wide shoulders that she was desperate to put her thighs on. He was thick but the waist of his navy-blue shirt was tucked neatly into his slacks, showcasing a chest and abdomen that were heavily muscled beneath a layer of softness around his middle. His arms were thick with muscle as they strained against the fabric of his shirt. He was built like one of those guys from a strong-man competition. The kind that carried boulders, tossed entire tree trunks, dragged semi-trucks... He was just *big*.

Van towered over her from behind. He was tall and lean and strong, with a litheness like a basketball player. She wanted to climb him like a goddamn tree.

The elevator dinged and she panted as Grant released her mouth from the bruising kiss. She was so wet she was aching. Van's hand in her hair disappeared as Grant led her from the elevator and she felt the loss of his touch in her soul.

"Which room?" Grant asked thickly.

"Five-Oh-Nine," Hope breathed, pointing down the hall to their right.

Grant secured her hand in his as they made their way down the hallway, Van trailing behind. Glancing back, she saw him several steps behind, his hands shoved into the front pockets of his slacks. His gaze was locked on her ass, swaying and jiggling slightly as she walked ahead of him, and she blushed, worry and self-consciousness clouding her thoughts briefly. Then her eyes dropped, and her mouth fell open when she saw the bulge at the fly of his slacks. She licked her lips and raised her eyes back to his, finding him staring at her with a feral, hungry look in those green depths. She reached her hand out behind her toward him, gesturing for him to take it.

He smirked at her, his blonde hair falling over his brow and she wanted to push it back with her fingers. He reached forward and clasped her hand as they made their way to her room.

Loathe to lose contact with either of them, she hurriedly snatched the keycard out of a hidden pocket in her dress and swiped it. The whirring of the lock as it disengaged was the only sound out in the deserted hallway except for their breathing.

Pushing the door open, she backed into it, followed closely by the two. As soon as the door clicked shut, Van's hands were lost in her hair and hauling her against him, his mouth closing over hers voraciously. Grant stepped behind her and splayed his hands wide on her ass, cupping the heavy swell of each cheek as he lowered his mouth to the exposed skin at the crook of her neck and shoulder. Her fingers fisted in Van's shirt, pulling him closer even as she ground her ass backward against Grant's hands. His hands splayed wide, his fingers digging into the softness on the side of her hips, his thumbs in the plumpness of her ass as he pulled her back against him, grinding his cock against her. She moaned brokenly.

"Ohhh," she breathed against Van's mouth.

"Fuck, this ass," Grant growled, his mouth leaving her neck and she felt him lean away, and she knew he was staring at her ass as it rested against his lap. He gave it a sharp slap and her entire body melted. "So fucking sexy."

Van left her mouth, and she bit her lip, staring up at him through hooded eyes. His thumb rubbed along her lower lip. "I'm going to fuck this mouth, little one. Yes?"

She nodded, still gazing up at him. Her eyes fluttered closed when Grant ground himself against her ass again, his arm snaking around her middle to hold her closer. His voice was husky against her ear, and she felt his chest rumble against her back as he murmured, "You're being such a good girl for us. I want this dress off and then I want you to sit on my face while you suck his cock."

"Holy shit," she panted, letting her head drop back against Grant's chest. His other hand slid around her throat, closing over her jaw and turning her face toward his so he could kiss her.

He released her, stepping back far enough to find the zipper of the dress. Wasting no time, he lowered it, then peeled the dress off her upper body, shoving it over her wide hips until it fell to the floor at her feet. She stepped out of it and kicked her heels off, sinking down several inches.

Van's eyes traveled over her and she felt his appreciation as he took in her underwear. A black bustier corset bra pushed her tits up and cinched in her waist. A matching black thong covered just enough of her front to keep him from getting a full view of her pussy. The softness of her body was showcased now that the dress was off, the bustier bra pushing the squishiness of her middle down. She almost covered the bare skin of her stomach between the bottom of the bustier and her panties with her hands, but the look on Van's face convinced her not to. He liked what he saw.

"Jesus your body should be illegal," Van breathed, running the backs of his fingers along the exaggerated curves of her breast, waist, and hip in the bustier. "Do you see how fucking gorgeous she is, Grant?"

"Mmhmm. So fucking pretty," Grant agreed from behind her, and a second later another sharp slap had been delivered to one of her ass cheeks and she moaned breathily. "Do you like that, baby girl? Do you like being spanked?"

"Oh fuck, yes," Hope gasped, and he did it again, this time her knees buckling before she caught herself. Then she felt Grant's fingers at her spine, flicking open the multiple clasps of her bustier until it fell to the floor, spilling her breasts. Lines from the tight corset marred her skin and Grant hummed in disapproval as he hooked his thumbs in her thong and shoved those down her thighs until she stepped out of them, too.

"As sexy as that thing is, I don't like seeing your skin marked up, baby girl," he breathed against the shell of her ear. "Unless it's from us."

He was gone then, and she heard the rustling of clothes behind her, and she watched as Van tugged the button-down shirt from the waistband of his slacks before tearing at the buttons. She was torn; her eyes flicking from one gorgeous man to the other. Two clinks of metal as belts were undone, the rasp of two zippers, and the rustling of clothes as they were shed were the only sounds she could hear above the pounding of her own heart.

Her eyes widened when they both stood naked in front of her. Van was long and thick, and she licked her lips at the thought of that in her mouth. And then she glanced at Grant, and she breathed out, "Oh fuck," when she saw the impossibly thick cock he was working with. "You two are going to ruin my vagina. And the rest of me for anyone else."

Grant chuckled and took her hand, leading her to the bed where he lowered himself to his back so that he lay diagonally across the bed. "Get up here, baby girl. I want my tongue in your pussy, now."

Not needing to be told twice, she climbed up, straddling his big chest, and his massive hands dug into her ass again, hauling her up closer to his mouth. She cried out in panic as she lost her balance, but Van was there in front of her, catching her. She was acutely, painfully aware of every jiggly inch of her that was on full display for these two insanely hot men.

"Sit," Van ordered, staring into her eyes. His hand smoothed over her hair before gripping the back of her head. "Sit down, Hope. He wants you to sit on his face."

"But—" she protested, moaning at the bite of pain from Grant's fingers as they dug into the thickest part of her thighs, urging her lower. She felt his breath on her pussy, and then his tongue as it slid along her wet opening. He groaned ferally beneath her, his arms banding around her thighs and forcing her to sit. His tongue delved into her and she shuddered, grinding herself against his mouth as he devoured her. "I don't want to hurt—"

Pushing her up just enough to free his mouth, Grant grunted darkly, "You're hovering. If I die between these thighs, I'll die a happy man. Now sit, butterfly. I won't tell you again."

His hands were unforgiving as he forced her to lower herself over him again, until his lips and tongue were right where she wanted him the most. "Ohmygod," she moaned, her eyes fluttering shut.

"Open your eyes, little one. Look at us," Van said then, pulling her attention back to him and away from the heaven that she'd fallen into with Grant licking and sucking her clit like it was his last meal. "Good girl. Now bend over and open those pretty lips for me."

She did as she was told, shifting and licking her lips in anticipation. "Please," she moaned, even as Grant continued to fuck her senseless with his tongue. Van fisted her hair in his hand and she opened her mouth, greedily sucking him in as he pushed the broad head of his cock into her mouth. Her fingers found purchase, holding on for dear life as Van sank his full length into her, all the way to the back of her throat. She gagged, tears streaming from her eyes, but she sucked greedily at him, taking him as far as she could with each thrust. Her entire body thrummed with need, and then—

Her mouth popped off Van's cock with a stuttered moan as Grant's tongue brought her to a body shaking orgasm; her thighs trembling violently on either side of his head. She sobbed, throwing her head back and panting desperately. She stared up at Van, his lips parted in awe and hunger as he watched her come apart.

The arms that were still banded around her thighs lifted her and then tossed her onto her back and she laughed breathlessly as she bounced on the bed. The laughter stopped when he followed, fitting his hips between her thighs. No man this large should move as lithely as he did. Van tossed a condom onto the bed beside them and Grant picked it up, tearing it open with his teeth before rolling it onto his dick.

"I'm going to fuck this pussy until I come, and then I'm going to watch Van fuck you, baby girl," he growled as he knelt between her thighs, draping them over his, his hands on her ass. "Open up for me."

Spreading her thighs wider, her mouth dropped open in a soundless moan when he pushed inside her in one long, hard thrust. He stretched her wide and her back bowed off the bed as he bottomed out, grinding into her. His hands spanned over her ass and hips, fingers digging in roughly as he began to move. Her eyes sought Van, who was standing beside the bed, stroking his own cock as he watched them. Her orgasm was tightening her stomach as it barreled toward her, and she sobbed as it overtook her like a freight train.

"So fucking beautiful," Grant groaned, his hips pounding into hers as he came, too. "Fuck, I've never come so hard, butterfly. Such a good fucking girl, coming for us."

She was still panting when he slid out of her, collapsing on the bed beside her. Van climbed onto the bed and flipped her over onto her stomach. "On your knees, ass in the air, little one."

Boneless, she tucked her knees under her, her chest flat on the bed. She heard another condom wrapper rip, and then without hesitation, Van was sliding into her from behind, all the way in. She gripped the sheets tight in her fingers, moaning long and low as he began to move. He hit deeper than Grant had, and her eyes rolled into the back of her head as her toes curled. The head of his cock hit her in that secret spot deep inside, and she sobbed brokenly when she felt Grant's hand between her thighs, his fingers flitting over her clit with a precision that should've been illegal.

Van's hips drove into hers, his fingers digging sharply into the fleshy curves of her waist until she was sure she would have bruises, but she didn't care, because he was fucking her into another mind shattering orgasm with Grant's fingers speeding it along. She could see that he was hard again, his other hand pumping rhythmically over his own cock even as his fingers flicked at her clit. Rising up onto the palms of her hands until her upper body came off the bed, she looked over at Grant and begged brokenly, "Grant. Kiss me."

Raising onto an elbow, he caught her mouth with his, silencing her scream even as it was torn from her throat. Her entire body shook violently as she came with an explosion around Van's cock.

"Yes, fuck," Van snarled from behind her. His fingers drifted down her spine as he picked up his pace, hammering into her, prolonging her orgasm as he chased his own. His hips stuttered and then she heard his feral groan as he came, too. Still, Grant continued kissing her senseless, and then she felt his teeth nip at her lower lip and heard his grunt as he came in his hand. "Jesus, Hope. You're fucking perfect, little one."

Grant pressed another kiss to her mouth before pulling away and she blushed when she saw his cum splattered across his abdomen and chest. He stood and crossed to the bathroom, then returned with a damp cloth, which he used to clean between her legs gently. She was completely boneless when he laid down beside her, tugging her into his arms. Snuggling against his chest, she reached behind her blindly until she found Van's hand, intertwining her fingers with his.

"Go to sleep, baby girl," Grant whispered against the crown of her head.

"Are you going to leave?" she asked quietly, almost afraid to put the question into words. "While I'm sleeping?"

"We'll be here when you wake, little one," Van said from behind her, squeezing her hand gently. And because her body was thoroughly exhausted from the soul-snatching orgasms they'd delivered, she fell asleep snuggled securely between them both.

Chapter Four

The locking mechanism on the door whirred to life, jolting her awake. She sat up, disoriented, and clutched the sheet to her chest between tight fingers as the door swung open. Her mouth fell open and she sighed with relief as Van, then Grant, stepped into the room, closing the door behind them. Van had a disposable coffee cup in his hand and a brown paper sack in the other. Grant carried two disposable coffee cups in his.

"Hi," she whispered shyly, wrapping the sheet more firmly around her naked torso where she still sat in the center of the bed. Aware that she must look like a fright, she reached up and tucked a strand of hair behind her ear, dropping her eyes to her lap self-consciously.

Grant sank onto the edge of the mattress, setting both coffees on the bedside table before sinking the fingers of one hand into the mess of her hair at the back of her head, pulling tight enough to make her look up at him. "Good morning, baby girl."

She swallowed hard. "Good morning," she whispered, her voice still husky from sleep.

Grant's other hand fisted into the sheet and yanked it away, revealing her nakedness to them. His hand slid between her thighs, fingers delving into her and she moaned, dropping her head back. His mouth traveled over the skin of her throat, her bare shoulder and then she felt the bed sink on her other side as Van sat beside her. His hand cupped her breast, his fingers tugging at her nipple. Grant twisted her head so that she was facing Van, and his mouth was on hers a heartbeat later.

"I thought you'd have snuck out while you had the chance," she whispered against his mouth, her chest tightening painfully at the thought.

"We said we wouldn't, and we're just getting started, little one," Van husked when he released her lips, and then she was being shoved lightly until she laid back on the bed. Van lowered his mouth to hers again and then she felt Grant spread her legs for him to situate himself between them. His large, rough hands squeezed the soft inner portion of her thighs, pinning them to the bed. She moaned loudly into Van's mouth when she felt Grant's breath as it ghosted over her pussy.

"That's right, butterfly, just lay back and let us take care of everything," Grant murmured before his lips closed over her clit, making her legs shake. "Because you're ours. Or did you forget already?"

"I think we need to remind her, Grant," Van hummed, his hand closing around her throat lightly. She writhed beneath the onslaught of Grant's magic tongue and Van's incredible fingers. "Remind our girl who she belongs to."

"My pleasure," Grant growled before diving back in, his tongue doing deliciously dirty things to her as Van's fingers tilted her face up to his once more, his mouth settling over hers in a deep, soul shattering kiss.

Oh yeah.

Best. Birthday. Ever.

Chapter Five

SIX WEEKS LATER

"Is this the last of it?"

Hope nodded, brushing a strand of hair out of her face with the back of her arm as best she could, laden with a moving box as it was. "Yes. This is all of it."

"Thank God," her sister huffed teasingly as they walked together up the short walkway to her sister's apartment. Her sister's ancient golden retriever, Bruno, padded slowly beside them, his muzzle heavy with white fur. "My apartment just shrunk by half."

"Hey, your plants take up half the apartment as is... And I don't have that much stuff!" Hope protested weakly, exhausted after the work of the day. "It all fit into my car. I left everything else with Tony and *Matthieu.*"

The name fell off her lips in a sneer and then she felt guilty all over again. It wasn't Matthieu's fault that her fiancé had hidden that he was bisexual for all of their relationship. Only coming out after meeting and falling in love with the young, handsome French pastry chef that moved in next door.

And at least Tony hadn't cheated... exactly. So much of their relationship made sense now, though. She set the last box down on the floor just inside the door. The pile of her things was all that she had left. It was an abysmal sight.

Jade, her older sister, turned and smiled gently. "You're allowed to be upset, Hope. You're too nice. You let them keep the apartment and all the stuff in it... after finding out your fiancé was in love with another man. You're a better person than I am."

Hope shrugged. "Who am I to stand in the way of true love? It's not like it was an issue that I could fix." Yeah. She was blessed with a vagina between her legs instead of a penis. Not exactly a 'reconcilable difference'. She snorted to herself.

"If he had cheated on you with a woman, would that have made a difference?" Jade asked.

Hope didn't have an answer for that. "He didn't cheat. At least, he says they didn't until after we'd split."

"But an emotional affair is just as bad, Hope, if not worse," Jade muttered, pulling a bottle of white wine out of the refrigerator and unscrewing the top—because they were classy bitches—and poured it into two mismatched wine goblets. She handed one to Hope, who took it and took a long swallow. What a day.

"I don't want to talk about Tony and Matthieu," she said and rolled her shoulders to alleviate the tension in them. After packing her car up that morning, driving the nine hours to get to her hometown in northern Michigan, and then unloading her vehicle... she was beat. Her body hurt. "I do, however, want to talk about that absolutely adorable guy that helped us unload my car..."

"Asher?" Jade laughed, taking a drink of her own wine.

"Wait, that was *Asher*? As in, Asher Phillips? Like, your bestie's little brother? *That Asher*?" Hope asked, her voice raising several octaves in shock. Jade nodded. She fanned herself and grinned over at her older sister. "Oooh boy. He grew up so good."

Jade snatched a plastic spatula out of the ramekin on the counter and threw it at her. "Shut up! He's still a baby!"

Hope used her fingers to count backwards, thinking, then grinned. "He's what, twenty-three, twenty-four now?"

"He's *a kid*, Hope," Jade chastised and rolled her eyes.

"That was no kid, my dearest sister," Hope laughed, waggling her eyebrows at her. "And he totally has the hots for you."

"Oh god, stop!" Jade moaned and clapped her hands over her ears, singing a loud *lalalalala* to drown Hope out. "You used to babysit him!"

Hope shrugged and grinned again. "I did not babysit him, I tutored him. And I'm not saying I want to go for him. But you totally should."

"This conversation is over," Jade laughed, giving a small shudder. "No. Absolutely not. He's so young, Hope. And I'm... old."

"You're thirty-one, that's hardly old, Jade," Hope muttered, leaning against the countertop on her forearms. "Shit, there had to be at least a dozen years between myself and Grant," she said, her throat seizing and his name coming out as more of a croak. Shit. She had done so well not thinking about him. Or Van. *Fuck.*

Rubbing her chest absentmindedly to ward off the ache that had begun to gnaw at her breastbone, she swallowed and changed the subject quickly, asking, "He just happened to stop by?"

"His parents still live down the street from here, he pops through every so often," Jade said, thankfully ignoring the mention of her wild weekend in Chicago. It sometimes felt like a dream. *Had she dreamed the whole thing?* "Want to watch a movie and binge on popcorn and wine?"

"Only if you have a bag of sour gummy worms hidden somewhere in one of these cabinets." Jade laughed, pointing toward one over the refrigerator. Hope bounced over to the cupboard and opened it, sighing, "Aha!" Plucking the bag of candy out, she opened it and popped a red and blue worm into her mouth with a smile.

They migrated to the small living room and settled into opposite ends of Jade's thrift store find couch; it was ugly as sin but comfortable to boot. Every window had multiple thriving houseplants in macrame plant hangers in front of them, and almost every inch of space above the kitchen cabinets had more greenery. Long hanging Pothos, trailing English Ivy that had taken up one side and climbed across to the window over the sink, leggy Spider Plants, and one absolutely ginormous, bushy fern that occupied one window all by itself. In one corner of the living room, a tall, staggered shelf unit housed another dozen potted plants. *Her sister needed to get laid*, she thought with a roll of her eyes.

Bruno climbed up onto the cushions between them and lay down with a huff, resting his wide, mostly white head in Jade's lap. Hope draped a fluffy blanket over her legs as Jade queued up *Roadhouse*. There was just something about Sam Elliot and his silver foxiness...

"So, did you ever find them?" her sister asked a while later, while Patrick Swayze was beating the stuffing out of some baddie in the dance hall.

Hope sighed, shaking her head. She wasn't sure she was ready to talk about that, either. "No. It's probably best that way."

"You could try to search for them on google? Or try Facebook?" her sister suggested, taking a drink of her wine.

"All I have are two first names," Hope said and shrugged. "I don't know where they're from, what kind of restaurant they own... With my luck, they're both married, and I had a crazy one-night stand with two very unavailable men who live on polar opposite sides of the country than me..."

"Technically it was a two-night stand..." Jade corrected, winking, and Hope rolled her eyes.

"Shut up," Hope laughed and threw a gummy worm at her sister, who caught it and popped it into her mouth. Bruno's eyebrows lifted, his eyes shifting to watch, but he didn't lift his head. Hope scratched his fluffy butt where it was pressed against her legs. "I'm still mad at myself for telling you."

"Why? I would die if you'd kept this from me! I haven't gotten any in so long there's probably cobwebs down there," Jade laughed. Hope groaned; she was right. Her sister needed to get laid, bad. "I have to live vicariously through you."

Hope swallowed the lump in her throat. She'd tried everything to forget them. But still she dreamed of them. Every night. And every morning she would wake up alone.

Because she had insisted on no last names. No hometowns. No personal information. That was the deal they made. One wild, crazy, passionate weekend. It was stupid to keep wishing things had been different. She couldn't go back and change it, now. No, she had to live with the fact that she would probably go the whole rest of her life and never find them. Would likely never find anything that even came close to what she'd found with them. And it sucked.

It had been six weeks since her birthday weekend in Chicago... six weeks since she'd left two of the hottest men she'd ever seen sleeping in her hotel room, and snuck out like a thief in the night. Only she wasn't the thief... they were. Because her heart had not been the same since. Besides, whatever had been started in that room between the three of them... it could never work in the real world.

And she'd had to leave before her poor heart could beg for them to try. Because dammit, she had wanted to try.

Which was crazy, right? Who fell like that for two strangers over the course of a weekend?

Hope did, that's who. And it hurt like hell every day since. Stupid, stupid heart. It had always been her downfall. She fell in love too easily. She was hopeless like that. She snorted to herself.

"We can find them," Jade suggested softly, as if reading Hope's thoughts.

She smiled over at her sister, then shook her head. "I can't go my whole life looking for two strangers, Jade. The likelihood of ever finding them is slim-to-none. I had a wonderful weekend, and that is what it is."

"Well, you're home now, and the Mackenzie sisters are back

together finally. This town doesn't know what's hit them yet," Jade teased.

"Damn right," Hope laughed, raising her wine glass toward her sister. They tapped their glasses together in a cheers.

"Any prospects on jobs?"

Nodding, Hope swallowed a drink of her wine and said, "Yes, actually. I have an application in with a pre-school that is looking to add another early childhood education teacher. It sounds hopeful, so I'm keeping my fingers crossed. They said they should have an answer for me by tomorrow."

"Well, if you get it, we have to go out and celebrate," Jade said, hauling herself off the couch to grab the bottle of wine from the kitchen. "I know your visits were never long enough for us to really go all out, and there's this restaurant that opened a couple years ago that is just *to die for*." Folding herself back into the corner of the couch, she topped off her wine glass and then reached out and did the same for Hope's. "The girls from work and I usually go on Friday nights anyway. They have live music, and they serve warm bread with oil and balsamic to dip it in."

"Ugh, I love bread," Hope groaned and laughed.

Jade laughed and once again gestured to herself and her curvy body. "Girl, same." Smiling at each other, Jade reached out and clasped Hope's hand with hers. "I'm glad you're home. I missed you."

"I missed you, too," she whispered, dragging a deep breath in and then letting it out as tears stung her nose. It was good to be home.

Chapter Six

His business partner was in his office chair, leaning forward, one hand bracing his chin with his elbow on the desk. He was staring at the computer in front of him when Sulivan Laurance walked in without knocking. Grant Price's eyes sliced up to him briefly before returning to the screen. Scrubbing a hand over his bearded face, he sighed, and Van leaned a shoulder against the doorjamb, crossing his arms over his chest.

"This sucks, man," Grant muttered darkly, shaking his head. Leaning back in the oversized office chair, he sighed again and raised his eyes to stare at the ceiling. "We have to fire him."

Van nodded from where he stood, one hip thrown out, his ankles crossed. He stared down at the floor. Fuck. They were fair and lenient bosses. More than fair. More than lenient. But stealing was stealing, and they had solid proof, as Grant had just found on their camera system.

"Stupid prick," Van muttered, shaking his head as he pushed away from the door. He crossed the carpeted floor and sank into a chair opposite Grant, reclining on his tailbone, legs outstretched in front of him. "How much?"

"Three bottles, over the course of as many months," Grant grumbled, leaning forward and placing a giant paw of a hand on the computer mouse, dragging it around. Van assumed he was replaying the video. "Fuck! I hate losing a good bartender."

"So what do we do? Do we want to try to hire someone before we let him go? Or just run short for a few weeks until we can find someone new?" Van asked, sitting up and bracing his elbows on his spread knees. This was shit news on a Friday morning.

"No, he needs to go, like yesterday," Grant grunted, shaking his head angrily. His dark hair had been pushed back from his forehead several times already with tense fingers. The silver seemed to stand out more in the early October daylight streaming through the window behind him. At least the summer rush was over, the summer tourists having left for their warmer climate homes until springtime the next year. "I'll pull Michelle off the floor and put her behind the bar with Jackson. The others will just have to absorb an extra table into their section, and I'll table-touch more throughout the evening to watch for any issues."

Van nodded, once again staring at the floor between his widespread feet. Working alongside his best friend was a blessing most days and a curse on the rare day. It wasn't often that they ever disagreed on anything, and luckily, they trusted each other enough to run their areas of the restaurant nearly seamlessly.

The last six weeks have been a struggle... Shaking his head, he dispelled the thought. He couldn't afford to fall down that rabbit hole again. It hadn't helped that he'd woken up that morning thinking about her. Again. Like every goddamn night before that. He knew that Grant was struggling just as he was.

Damn woman. *Hope.*

What a name for the woman that had left him with such a hopeless hole in his chest. What fucking irony.

Staring at Grant, Van assessed him. Older than Van by about six years, his dark hair was streaked heavily with silver, as was the thick beard that covered his face. Laugh lines etched at the corners of his dark eyes, rimmed with dark lashes that spiked away from his eyes. Built like a goddamn grizzly bear, he was big and beefy, but cuddly like a fucking panda. Kind and generous and sometimes much too willing to forgive transgressions. Though rarely, the man could hold a grudge like no other. When he leveled that dark, intense stare at someone, he could be more than a little intimidating.

He looked tired, withdrawn. Van knew his friend well, and though infrequent, he would sometimes fall into a black mood. He wondered if the last appointment hadn't gone well and made a mental note to ask about it later. Grant didn't like to discuss personal things in the office. Claimed there were too many ears. Which was true, and the rumor grapevine ran longer and faster than one of their vintage wine grape vines.

Or, like Van, maybe he was just miserable for a completely different reason. A blonde-haired, blue-eyed mystery girl reason.

They didn't talk about her, though. Never.

Sharing wasn't something that was new to them, just something they'd done a few times to break up the monotony. And it was fun. And hot. But they were always short flings and never meant anything more than just a few orgasms and a good time. Sharing didn't extend to women they dated. Grant had had girlfriends, as had he. And that was a line they'd never crossed.

But Hope… She'd changed everything. One fucking weekend with her and he was willing to try anything, if it had meant that he could keep her. He'd never put much stock in the whole 'soulmates' crock, but damn did he, now. He would've shared her, always, if that's what she'd wanted. If that's what Grant had wanted.

It was what he'd wanted, too.

Waking up that morning in Chicago and finding her gone had wrecked him. There was *before*. And there was *after*.

Neither of them was the same, after Hope.

Chapter Seven

The cork of the champagne bottle popped loudly, and Hope laughed as she set her purse down on the counter. Jade was already pouring the champagne into the same two mismatched wine glasses from the night she'd moved in. When Hope had gotten the call while out for coffee that she'd gotten the teaching job, she had immediately called Jade to share the good news.

"To my sister, the shaper of young minds!" Jade whooped, holding her champagne up for Hope to clink their glasses together.

Hope laughed, shaking her head. "I'm so glad I got this. I was worried moving after the school year started would make it tough to find a teaching position."

"We are *so* going out tonight!" her sister said, walking around the peninsula counter of the kitchen. Bruno was in his orthopedic dog bed on the floor, but he watched them as they walked around the room. "You have something to wear tonight?"

"To that one restaurant? How fancy are we talking?" Hope asked, drawing her eyebrows together in trepidation. Most of her clothes were still packed and buried in boxes in the corner.

"Dressy casual is fine," Jade said and waved her hand dismissively.

"Black jeans, black blouse, black cropped leather jacket?" Hope asked, eyeing the weather outside. Early and mid-October in northern Michigan usually meant chilly evenings, and she didn't like the idea of wearing a skirt or dress once the temperature dropped. "I think I know where a pair of black strappy heels are packed..."

"No, that's perfect," her sister said, sipping her champagne. She flitted around the room, wearing a matched set of light gray sweatpants and a cropped zippered hoodie. The zipper was only pulled halfway up, leaving a large swatch of exposed chest and cleavage. Sans bra, her large breasts swayed freely beneath the material of the hoodie. She had that exaggerated hourglass figure that most women would die for. Several inches of her belly were exposed as she moved, and a pair of fuzzy sandal slippers were on her feet. Her toenails were painted white, as were her fingernails. Her strawberry blonde hair was piled on top of her head in a messy topknot and her freckles seemed to stand out more than usual in the early afternoon sunlight streaming through the window. She was chaotically flawless in an annoyingly effortless way. "A few of the gals from work will be there, I hope that's okay."

"I really don't have to go, I feel like I'm crashing your girl time," Hope said, scrunching her face.

"Absolutely not," Jade laughed. "They're all looking forward to meeting you. They're cool. You'll like them, they'll like you, I promise. So stop being weird."

"What time are we supposed to be meeting your friends?" she asked, changing the subject.

Jade glanced at the clock. "In about an hour and a half. Is that enough time?"

Hope grimaced. "If I can locate my clothes and those black heels, sure."

"Well then get moving."

"I'm not the one still in my pajamas—"

"Umm, okay, sassy pants. I had a short day at work today, and no, I'm not going to wear a skintight sports bra once I'm home. That thing is a torture device and it had to go," Jade laughed and propped her hands on her hips. "So damn straight I'm back in comfy clothes. And I'll still be ready before you are."

"No way. You take two hours to get ready."

"I'll take that bet," Jade sing-songed, sashaying away into the bedroom on the other side of the living room. "And I'll even be ready in less than an hour and a half. If I win, you have to at least attempt to google search for your mystery men."

Hope rolled her eyes again. "You're on."

One hour and twenty-seven minutes later, Jade was tapping the toes of one of her black, thigh high boots as she stood by the door... waiting for Hope. A rust brown, corduroy mini skirt covered very little of her upper thighs above the thigh high boots. She had pulled on a simple charcoal gray top and had topped it with a buttery soft duster sweater in the same charcoal gray color. The hem of the duster sweater swished around her calves; her strawberry blonde hair styled loose around her shoulders. Her sister was gorgeous.

Hope huffed in annoyance and pulled on her cropped black leather jacket, pulling her long blonde hair out of the back. "Okay. You win. Stop tapping your foot at me."

"You're so google searching them later," Jade chuckled. "I'll have the girls help, if you want them to—"

"No!" Hope exclaimed, then blushed furiously. "No, Jade. I don't need anyone else knowing I had a three way with two strangers while on vacation after being dumped. Please."

Jade held up her hands in surrender and Hope nodded in thanks. Making a full 360-degree turn, she asked, "So? Will this work? I couldn't find the blouse I wanted—"

"Smokin' hot," Jade said and winked. "That top is great. Where are those jeans from?"

"Uhh, they're Judy Blue's, I think," she said, glancing down at the body-hugging black jeans. Small tears in the knees and across one thigh gave them an edgy vibe. Paired with the black strappy, chunky heels, and a simple black, scoop neck t-shirt that hugged every curve from hip to chest. She felt sexy while still being comfortable. Her blonde hair had been left down and she'd even used a curling iron to put a little wave in the long locks. Simple make up adorned her face, but a vibrant red lip made her feel fearless. At least for a little while.

Jade scratched Bruno's head, they said good-bye to the old dog, and then Jade slid her arm through Hope's as they exited the apartment. Climbing into the passenger seat of Jade's car, she said, "I'm so ready for a drink. Where are we going, by the way?"

"It's called *The Wine Garden*," Jade said, turning down a side street and aiming them in the direction of Petoskey's downtown gaslight district. "Phenomenal wine list."

"Well, I would hope so," Hope laughed, shaking her head. It only took a few minutes for them to reach their destination, and when Jade parallel parked in front of a cozy looking restaurant with a brick paved walkway lined with wrought iron lanterns, Hope nodded in appreciation. There was a small patio off to one side of the building, but with the sun going down across the bay, the temperature was dropping, so no one was sitting outside.

They exited the car and walked toward the heavy wooden door and entered. A young hostess in a chic black dress greeted them from a small hostess stand just inside the door.

"Good evening, Jade. How many in your party tonight?" the girl asked, smiling kindly at them, her eyes bouncing from Jade to Hope. Her hands hovered over a stack of leather-bound menus.

"The usual, plus one," Jade said with a laugh. "So six of us. Thank you, Jenny."

The young woman smiled and nodded, plucking up the menus. "Perfect. Right this way, Mr. Price has your table ready, as usual."

"The man is as wonderful as they get," Jade laughed, following the hostess toward a round table in the center of the room. A giant stone fireplace sat against one wall, a small fire glowing in the hearth.

"I do have to tell you, please be patient this evening, we are down a waitress, so the other servers had to take on an extra table each for the evening," the young woman said as she set the menus down on the table.

"We'll be on our best behavior," Jade promised with a wink. The young lady laughed.

"Thank you," the hostess said with another smile, then nodded toward the kitchen. "It's been a... well, it's been a day." She leaned down close and whispered conspiratorially, "This is on the down low, but Mr. Price and Chef had to fire someone today, so he's grumpier than usual."

Jade gasped, looking around, then whispered back, "Who?"

Hope stared raptly between her sister and the hostess, who glanced around once again before whispering, "Nolan, the bartender. I guess he was stealing booze."

"Nooooo..." Jade breathed, her eyes wide. Hope wanted to laugh. "That's crazy! Well, thanks for sharing the drama, sis!"

"You ladies make my Friday nights better," the hostess said and laughed, finally straightening. "I'll send the other ladies over as soon as they get here. Teresa will be over in just a few minutes."

"Thank you," Hope and Jade murmured at the same time, smiling. When the hostess walked away, Jade laughed.

"Gosh, I do not miss the drama of restaurant work," she laughed, shaking her head. "So glad I didn't have to go back to waiting tables after finishing my classes."

"How is work going, anyway? Do you still like it?" Hope asked, taking a sip of the lemon water in front of her. It was icy and delicious on her tongue.

"I love it, and I get to split my time between the salon and the gym," her sister said with a smile. "Salon perks and a free gym membership? Shoot, I get the best of both worlds. And I get to work with some really awesome people at both places. Let me tell you, the eye candy in the gym... phew! There are these two sheriff's deputies that come in... They're so stupidly hot, it's not even fair."

Hope laughed. "You've always been boy crazy. I'm sure working in a gym with a bunch of hot men doesn't help."

Jade waved her hand and rolled her eyes. "Whatever. I don't mix business with pleasure. That's a strict rule I follow. Too messy. But they are nice to look at." She sighed then. "Sometimes it's hard, you know? I walk in and I get so many nasty looks. A girl my size in the gym?" She snorted, before taking a drink of her own water. "You'd think me being there is a personal offense to them."

"Well, that's their own problem, not yours," Hope muttered. "And when they get hurt and need a massage, who is going to help them? You are. Because you're a better person than they are. Size doesn't determine someone's worth. You know that, right?"

"Of course," Jade scoffed, but she smiled. Gesturing to herself, she winked and whispered, "I haven't had any complaints in the sex department. Ugh, not that I've had any in for-freaking-ever."

"Oh god," Hope laughed, cringing. "I don't want to know any details."

A waitress dressed in black slacks, a crisp white button-down shirt, and a long black apron stopped at their table. "Hello, how are you this evening? What can I get you two ladies started with to drink?"

"Cabernet for me, please," Jade said without hesitation, not even flipping open the drink menu. Smiling up at the waitress, she continued, "And I know we want to start with the olive oil and balsamic crostini's, please!"

Teresa laughed and nodded. "Of course. I'll bring extra over; I think I saw Keri and Bailey walk in when I was on my way over here. What can I get you to drink?" she asked Hope, who was busy scanning the wine list.

"I think a glass of the Butterfly Riesling sounds wonderful," she said, flipping the menu closed. *Butterfly*. She smiled up at the waitress, who nodded. "Thank you so much."

"Of course," Teresa said and smiled again. Addressing them both, she said, "As soon as the other gals arrive, I'll come back and go over tonight's specials."

"Perfect," Jade called softly, laughing. "Thank you!"

The waitress retreated, leaving Hope and Jade alone for only a moment before two women joined them at the table, sinking into chairs with warm hellos. Introductions were made, and before Teresa was back with their wines, two more ladies showed up, taking the last two seats. Hope learned that three of the women worked with Jade at the salon and the other one worked with her at the gym as a personal trainer.

When they all had ordered drinks and the bread with olive oil and balsamic glaze had been delivered to the table, they settled into easy conversation. They all seemed fun and friendly, and Hope found herself enjoying herself immensely. Dinner was served and they dug in ravenously. Jade had been right; this place was to die for.

Teresa brought a fresh glass of wine and Hope sipped it. She was having a good time for the first time in what felt like too long. Taking a large swallow of her wine, she welcomed the heat that bloomed across her cheeks, just buzzed enough to feel relaxed and happy. She almost forgot to think about Van and Grant. Almost.

"Oohh, there's Price," one of Jade's friends whispered, gesturing across the room. Hope glanced around, just barely seeing a broad set of shoulders pass from the hostess stand toward the kitchen before disappearing through the swinging door. "It's like they interviewed for hottest bosses or something for this place. I'd never get anything done if I worked here. I'd just stare at them both all the time."

"I hope Chef makes an appearance tonight," another friend said wistfully, glancing at the doors that led to the commercial kitchen in the back.

"He usually does, at least at some point," Jade said and nodded. Speaking to Hope, she said, "He's so hot, Hope. Like, ugh. *So hot.*"

The other ladies laughed and agreed. Hope's throat seized and she smiled the best she could. She missed *her* hot chef.

Chapter Eight

A headache was starting at the base of his skull, and Grant pinched the bridge of his nose between his forefinger and thumb. It had been one hell of a day. Firing Nolan, who threw a tantrum to rival a toddler, had just been the start. Reworking the floor plan for the evening after pulling Michelle off the rotation and putting her behind the bar was easy, his staff was competent and—for the most part—trustworthy.

Making his way out of his office and down a short hallway, he pushed open the door that led to the main room of the restaurant. It was a decently busy Friday evening, despite the fact that they were finally out of their busy season now that the majority of the tourists had taken their leave. From October to April, the little city of Petoskey got a reprieve from the influx of tourists and vacationers. It was always a much-needed rest before they all returned for the summertime.

Nodding to Michelle and Jackson behind the bar, he made his way toward the hostess stand to check on Jenny. She was young, barely eighteen, but handled the front with surprising efficiency. He rarely had to worry about her, but wanted to check in nonetheless.

Rolling his shoulders beneath the nearly black, dark aubergine purple button down he had on, he was glad he'd forgone the tie for the evening. Reaching up, he unbuttoned the second button at his throat. The sleeves were already rolled to his forearms, ready to assist wherever needed for the night. Dark gray slacks and black shoes completed the outfit, though he couldn't wait to get home and finally get into something more comfortable. And pour a hefty tumbler of bourbon.

Had he mentioned it had been a day?

"Jenny," he said gently as he came up behind the young girl, who turned and smiled hesitantly. He'd snapped at her earlier in the evening and felt like an absolute ass about it. "How is everything going tonight? No issues?"

"None at all, Mr. Price," Jenny said, her smile faltering slightly. He cursed himself again. He wasn't the asshole boss, but this day... shit, this *week*... had been a hellish one. "It's been smooth sailing. We've got this."

"Good," he said and winked. He liked Jenny. She reminded him of his niece, who he didn't get to see nearly often enough. He made a mental note to send her home with one of Van's Crème Brule's as an apology. "I'll go check on the kitchen. Find me if you need anything."

She nodded, dropping her eyes from his. *Dammit, he felt like a heel*. He turned and headed toward the kitchen. Their regular group of ladies laughed from the center of the room and he glanced over briefly before continuing to the kitchen to check on Van.

Pushing into the kitchen, he assessed the room. Organized chaos, is what Van called it. His business partner and best friend stood on this side of the metal expo rail, white chef jacket pristine as always, his blonde hair pushed back away from his face. He was calling orders out while garnishing a plate before turning and handing it to a waitress, who disappeared with it back out the kitchen doors. Van nodded at him as he made his way through the kitchen, then turned back to his staff.

"I need that lambchop, Derek," Van called across the line to a redheaded cook, who nodded.

"Yes, Chef," he called back, pulling the lambchop out of the pan and placing it on a white square plate, before passing it to Van.

"Looks great," Van said.

Derek nodded again and said, "Thank you, Chef."

Another waitress zipped past, carrying a charred romaine salad topped with feta, roasted apple, and toasted cinnamon pecans in one hand. The lambchop with Van's famous duchess potatoes and roasted Brussel sprouts drizzled with balsamic in the other. They smelled delicious and looked beautiful on the plate, as always.

"Everything going alright back here?" Grant asked Van as he stepped up beside him.

"Easy Friday night," Van said, glancing at him briefly. Van had given him wide berth for the day and he hated himself all over again. He was never the asshole, but damn had today made him grouchy. "How's it going out there?"

"Just about to do a round of table touches," Grant said, and Van nodded. "Call if you need anything."

"We're good back here," Van said, and Grant sighed, nodding.

He made his way back out of the kitchen, several servers and kitchen staff moving out of his way, eyes lowered to the floor. He'd made an example out of Nolan earlier, reminding the staff that though they were all valued and important, theft would not be tolerated, period. It had made for a very subdued pre-dinner call, which was normally filled with laughter and excitement before the dinner shift began.

Pushing back through the doors, he took a deep breath in and exhaled slowly, straightening his shoulders as he mentally prepared for the next several hours of interactions with customers. Stopping at a table nearest him, he said hello, greeted them by name, and asked how their meal was. Small talk followed, and then he excused himself to move on to the next table.

He had made it halfway through the tables when he glanced over toward the center of the room, and his heart did an awful beat skip in his chest, before hammering so hard it made his breath ragged.

Because there she was, sitting at a table in the center of the room, blonde hair tossed over her shoulder and a glass of wine at her smiling lips.

Her cheeks were slightly flushed, and he wondered how many glasses of wine she'd consumed. He noticed several of the women had already finished their meals, their plates having been cleared away. How long had she been sitting here? In his restaurant? And he'd had no idea?

He swallowed hard past the lump in his throat as he stared at her in profile. It had been six hellish weeks since he'd seen her after only spending a very short amount of time together, but he knew it was her. Knew it without a second of doubt. She smiled at something one of the other women said and it made his chest ache. She looked the same. And so fucking beautiful it hurt.

Fury so potent it made his ears ring crashed through him then. She was *here. In his fucking restaurant.* After running out of that hotel room in the middle of the night, leaving him with a hole in his chest that he hadn't even thought was possible after such a short amount of time. Something inside him had broken that morning, waking to find her gone. And now she was here.

And he was so *goddamn angry.* His body fairly shook with the rage simmering beneath his skin, through his chest. His fingers tingled and he shoved his hands into his pockets to hide the shaking.

Stalking over to the table and coming up behind her, he forced his fury down and he attempted to steel his features into a mask of pleasant aloofness. He just prayed his face didn't reveal just how close to losing it he was.

"Hello, ladies. How is everything this evening?" he asked, kicking himself for the uneven gruffness in his voice. He held his breath when he saw her go completely still.

That's right. Found you, butterfly.

Chapter Nine

Oh God.

That voice. *His* voice. She would know it anywhere. It still featured heavily in her dreams every night.

Grant.

Her mouth popped open in shock. She felt the blood rush from her face and the sensation of a rug being yanked out from beneath her feet made her sway in her seat. *He's here! Why was he here?* His voice was so even and cordial, absolutely no hint of recognition. *Did he not know it was her, even though she would know his voice from anywhere? Was she the only one having a major life crisis sitting here in this restaurant?* Anxiety made her feel panicky.

Barely daring to breathe, she swallowed the knot that had lodged in her throat, and she raised her eyes to his face from beneath her lashes. Her heart hammered in her chest so hard she was sure she was going to faint. The blood rushing through her head was so loud she couldn't tell if he was speaking, if Jade had answered his question... maybe she was having a stroke?

When her eyes finally landed on his face, her heart lurched

painfully. He looked remarkably the same; same dark hair and thick beard threaded through heavily with silver, same beautiful, kissable mouth and straight, aristocratic nose. Same well-fitted, dark button-down shirt that did little to hide the thick, heavy muscles that filled out his body. Same dark slacks fitted to tree trunk thighs. And when she finally had the courage to raise her eyes to his... *oh.*

If his facial expression and tone of voice were cordial... his eyes were decidedly *not.*

For the second time in as many minutes, she felt the blood drain from her face. He looked *pissed.* And those dark, coffee brown eyes were staring directly at her. *So, he does recognize me,* she thought weakly. *Great.*

"Everything is wonderful," her sister said, and Hope could hear the smile in her voice. The other girls at the table agreed, greeting him with appreciative smiles.

She was unable to look away from his face, his dark eyes so intense and angry as he stared down at her. Tears stung her nose for no other reason than she didn't like confrontation, and the way he was staring at her as though he hated her... it felt like a knife digging into her stomach and being twisted sharply.

Hope had regretted leaving the hotel room the second the door had closed, but she'd refused to knock to be let back in or go down to the desk to claim she'd lost her keycard to get a new one to let herself back into the room... to climb back into the wide bed between the two of them, to never leave. She had thought of him, of Van, of that weekend, for weeks. She *still* thought about them, constantly. How could she have known they were from her very own hometown? A home she hadn't visited for longer than a single weekend in years... Certainly she hadn't been home enough to warrant a dinner out to a fancy restaurant. All this time... and they'd been right here.

She'd had no idea where they lived, where they ran their restaurant. They could have been from anywhere in the US for heaven's sake. They could have lied about the whole thing, for all she knew. Her life had been turned upside down the week before she met them... and there was still the very real possibility that they were both married, or had families that they had kept hidden, or or or...

That's what she'd told herself anyway, in the days and weeks that had turned into nearly two months after leaving that hotel room. After walking away from the best weekend of her entire life. She'd told herself she would never see them again, that they wouldn't have been able to make it work. What kind of woman thinks about 'making it work' with the *two men* she had an impossibly sexy one night—er, *two night*—stand with anyway?

But oh god, seeing him now... the sting of tears in her nose overflowed into her eyes and she blinked rapidly to dispel them. She'd missed him. Even if he was angry to see her.

She lowered her gaze from his face to the glass of wine in front of her which began to waver slightly as the tears she unsuccessfully tried to hold in blurred her vision. Jade thanked him, and after a second longer, she saw out of her peripheral vision when he walked away from their table, disappearing through the kitchen door that swished shut behind him.

Dropping her napkin onto the table, she jumped to her feet, startling Jade so badly she sloshed her wine over the rim of her glass. "Whoa! Hope, are you okay? What's wrong?"

Snatching her purse up, she shook her head, unable to speak past the tears seizing her throat. Fingers fumbling, she opened her purse and pulled out cash, handing it shakily to her sister, who took it more out of shock than anything. She needed to run. Now.

She'd spent so many nights missing them. Missing him. Wishing she knew how to find them. And now she had, and it was a total disaster.

"I'm sorry," she whispered, her voice breaking. She tried to smile at her sister, at her sister's coworkers that she had just met. "I have to go. I'll see you at home."

"Hope—" her sister exclaimed in shock, but Hope was already weaving her way out of the restaurant.

She managed to make it past the hostess and out the heavy wooden doors that led out onto the brick paved walkway before the tears started to fall. Her chest was so tight she couldn't breathe. The neckline of her blouse suddenly felt suffocating, and she tugged at it to pull it away from her chest. Turning down the sidewalk, she didn't even bother walking to Jade's car, needing to escape. The tunnel that traveled beneath the small highway that dissected the downtown district and the Bay Front Park was only fifty feet away and she hurried toward it. She didn't even notice the chill in the air, racing away from the restaurant in the darkness that was only alleviated by the evenly spaced wrought iron light posts along the way.

When she reached the tunnel, it was blessedly empty, though she knew even in the fall there would be plenty of pedestrian traffic through the underground tunnel and she couldn't count on being undiscovered for long by a passerby. Shaking uncontrollably, she stopped walking, a sob breaking free of her throat. Leaning her back against the cool concrete that built the walls of the tunnel, she heaved a breath between sobs, burying her face in her hands.

Running footsteps echoed in the tunnel, and she sucked in a breath at an attempt to steady her breathing and quiet the sobs. Keeping her face averted, she swiped at the tears that tracked down her face. She prayed the pedestrian would just let her be, she didn't want to have to explain her tears to a stranger. Even a kind and helpful one.

Strong, gentle hands gripped her shoulders and spun her around, making her gasp in shock a heartbeat before arms were banded around her fiercely. Her face was pressed into a hard chest, one of those hands cradling the back of her head, fingers sliding through her hair.

"*What are you doing here?*" she heard the reverent whisper

against the top of her head just as the scent of olive oil and lemons pricked her nose. Hiccupping a sob, the tears started all over again.

Van.

Her fingers fisted into the fabric of his chef jacket as she buried her face in his chest, her shoulders shaking with her tears. The fingers in her hair smoothed gently, soothingly, which did nothing but make her cry all the harder. He was here. He was here and she was in his arms. *She'd found them.*

"I can't believe you're here... I hated myself the second I closed that hotel door," she tried to explain between hiccups, doing her best to take in a steadying breath. She didn't care if she sounded clingy, or desperate, or simply *crazy*. He was here and he was holding her. He shushed her gently, smoothing his hands over her hair again. The blatant anger she'd seen on Grant's face made her lower lip wobble again uncontrollably. "He's mad at me, isn't he."

She felt more than heard Van's soft chuckle beneath her ear, then felt his lips press against her temple, right at her hairline. His fingers continued to smooth over her hair. *God that felt so good. So familiar.* "Yeah, he is. We were both pretty mad at you."

She swallowed hard, taking a deep breath in. "I'm sorry." Her lip wobbled again. There was so much to say...

"We have plenty of time to talk, little one. Right now, I need to get you somewhere quiet so I can get back to my kitchen staff."

She let out a sad half laugh and drew away, averting her face and reaching to swipe away the remaining tears that streaked down her cheeks. She knew her face had to be a disaster. This was not the way she had imagined seeing him again for the first time.

But Van was having none of it, circling her wrists with his long fingers and drawing them away from her face before tipping her chin up. Embarrassed, she tried to dodge his hand, but he was insistent. She watched as his eyes roved over her face, taking in every single detail, before dropping his forehead to hers. "I never thought I'd get to see you again. Please...don't hide from me."

The sound of tapping heels and a panicked, "Get away from

her!" made Hope jump, moving to peer around Van's shoulder. Jade rushed toward them, arm outstretched with what looked like a compact aerosol can of hairspray clutched in her hand, aimed at Van. "I'm warning you!"

Hope let out a strangled laugh that was half hiccup, stepping around Van. Holding her hands up, she said, "It's okay. I'm okay. He's not hurting me."

Jade shook like a leaf as she stopped several feet away, arm still outstretched. Her eyes bounced from Hope's to Van's and back. "H-he wasn't hurting you?"

"No," Hope said softly and blushed, looking over at Van. "This is my sister. I kind of ran out on her at the restaurant."

"*Kind of?*" Jade shrieked, finally dropping her arm to her side, eyes wide, strawberry blonde hair wild around her head. "You scared the shit out of me, dammit!" Then, glaring up at Van, she demanded, "And just who the hell are you?"

"Jade... this is *Van*," Hope murmured quietly, staring at her sister intently, trying to communicate with her eyes. "We met in Chicago."

"Chicago..." Jade mouthed the word as her eyes went wide. "Oh. *Oh!*"

"And the man that stopped at our table..." she prompted, praying that her sister understood what she was saying without having to say the words. "His business partner..."

Jade opened her mouth to say something, closed it, then opened it again, nothing but a squeak coming out. "Holy shit," she breathed finally, still stunned nearly speechless.

Van stepped forward, offering his hand. Jade extended her own, placing it in his. Hope wanted to laugh at the incredulity on her sister's face, but the entire situation was still blowing her own mind. *They were here.*

"I apologize for Grant upsetting Hope. I have to admit, it shocked us both to find her here, too," Van said in that low, gentle voice of his. Hope blushed again when his gaze met hers and he smiled, before returning to her sister. "It's nice to meet you. Hope talked about you in Chicago."

"Right..." Jade murmured, drawing out the word, her eyes bouncing from Hope's to Van's again. She swallowed hard, as if trying to swallow her own tongue. "*Chicago*."

Hope blushed a furious shade of red and wished for the ground beneath them to open up and swallow her. "Jade! Why don't you go back into your dinner, I think I'm going to head home. I'll take an Uber. Let Van get back to work..."

Jade laughed then, shaking her head. "You're back in Kansas, Toto. Petoskey doesn't have Ubers."

"She's right, at least no reliable ones," Van said, sliding his hand along the curve of her back, just above her hips. The warmth of his hand through her top made her shiver. "You can come back to the restaurant. I'll set you up in my office and bring in a cup of coffee, or a glass of wine, whatever you want."

"But Grant—"

"He will come around," Van whispered, searching her eyes with his. The emerald green of his eyes was fringed with blonde lashes. She could stare at him for a lifetime and never get tired of looking at him. "Please, Hope. Don't make me say good-bye yet."

Chapter Ten

Heart still pounding erratically in his chest, Van escorted both women back through the tunnel and up the sidewalk toward the restaurant.

When Grant had stepped into the kitchen and said his name, Van had held up a finger, in the middle of speaking to his cooks on the other side of the line. He'd felt Grant step up next to him, but had ignored him until he was done giving instructions.

"*Van—*" Grant had grated, the deep, gravelly tone of his voice breaking through his concentration. Turning to look at him, panic had assailed him at the whiteness of his friend's face. Like he'd seen a ghost, or was ready to pass out. *Fuck, was it—*

Reaching one hand out, he demanded, "Grant, are you okay—"

But Grant had shaken his head, pinning him with a stare that could level a room. "*Hope.*"

If he hadn't known any better, he could have sworn that his heart had stopped as he'd stared at his friend, their eyes having more of a conversation than their mouths. "Where?"

"Table fifteen."

Pushing past Grant, he'd fairly sprinted out of the kitchen. He

DANIELLE BAKER

beelined for table fifteen, but didn't see anyone with long blonde hair at the table. Turning in a circle, his eyes scanned every single face in the room. Anxiety made his chest tight. Not seeing her, he'd rushed back to the kitchen, dragging Grant away from everyone else. "She's not out there. Are you fucking sure?"

Grant shoved at his chest, hard enough to knock him back but not enough to send him sprawling. "Yes, I'm fucking sure! She was here."

Spearing the fingers of both hands up through his hair, he swore, turning to put his back to Grant. Addressing the kitchen as a whole, he shouted, "Derek is in charge, I'll be right back!"

A chorus of "Yes, Chef" rang out and he nodded before exiting the kitchen again.

Striding to the hostess stand, he'd asked, "A woman with blonde hair, did she just leave?"

Jenny nodded, pointing to the door. "I think I saw her go right, Chef. Is everything okay? Is she in trouble?"

"Everything's fine," he called, rushing out the heavy wooden door and down the brick paved walkway to the sidewalk. Turning right, he jogged, glancing every direction, looking inside parked cars as he passed. Up ahead, the tunnel that burrowed beneath the highway separating the gaslight district and the Bay Front Park was lit from inside. As he got closer, his chest seized when he could hear the deep, wracking sobs that echoed from inside, and he rushed forward. Rounding the corner into the tunnel, he'd stumbled at seeing her for the first time in six weeks.

And then he'd had her in his arms. Heard her voice, felt her body beneath his hands, against his chest, smelled the blueberry and honey scent of her. Nothing had prepared him for seeing her again.

Now, as he walked the two women toward the restaurant, Hope stopped at the walkway toward the front door, and he sensed her panic without her saying a word.

"We can go in through the back," he said gently, his hand never leaving hers. He looked over to her sister. "I'll take care of her. Please, enjoy your evening with the girls. I'll inform your server that your table's tab is on me, tonight."

"No, that's really not necessary—" Hope's sister protested, but he raised his eyebrow and she stopped, before saying, "Thank you. That is very kind of you. The other ladies will be smitten."

She reached out and squeezed Hope's other hand, staring at her for a long time before releasing it and heading back into the restaurant. Van raised her fingers to his mouth, pressing his lips to the back of her fingers briefly. "Come on. I'll sneak you in the back."

They made it into the back side of the restaurant without encountering anyone else, to which he was grateful for, if only to give Hope the chance to collect herself.

His brain still hadn't completely wrapped around the fact that she was here, standing with him, her hand tucked into his. He could smell her, feel the heat of her skin against his. He was terrified that if he closed his eyes, if he even so much as blinked, she would disappear. That somehow maybe he'd had a psychotic break and was hallucinating the entire thing.

Opening the door to his small office, he entered, pulling her with him. One lamp had been left on where it sat in the corner of the room. "Have a seat, little one. I'll be right back."

She nodded, staring at him with those wide blue eyes. He smiled gently and cupped her cheeks in both of his hands, stroking his thumbs over her cheekbones. He leaned down and pressed a kiss to her forehead, lingering for a long heartbeat, before pulling away and stepping back.

Stepping out of the office, he made it down the hallway and opened the door to the main restaurant. Skirting the tables quickly, he stepped toward the bar and when Jackson, their head bartender, noticed him he hurried over. "Chef, what do you need?"

"A glass of water and a cup of coffee. Use the French vanilla cream, please," he said, pushing his fingers up through his hair, remembering how she liked her coffee from Chicago. He glanced around. "Where's Grant?"

Jackson was already working on the water and then stepped back to pour a cup of coffee. Van watched as he swallowed hard. Not good. "I'm not sure, Chef. He was in the kitchen last I knew. He uh... he made Jenny cry."

"Fuck," Van muttered and shook his head. He picked up the water and coffee. "Okay. I'll find him. Thank you."

"Thank you, Chef," Jackson said and then turned back toward another customer as Van rushed back the way he'd just came, pushing the door open and striding down the hallway.

He found Hope still standing in the center of the room, gazing around the small office. He set the water and coffee down on the desk. "Here, little one. I'm sorry I can't stay. I'll be back just as quick as I can. Have a seat."

"I really am sorry," she whispered and his heart ached when her lower lip wobbled again. She wrung her hands together in front of her, dropping her eyes to the floor. "I know I shouldn't say it, but I missed you so much, Van."

"Why shouldn't you say it?" he asked, reaching out and taking her hands in his. She was so soft. So pretty.

"Because it's *crazy*," she whispered miserably. "This whole thing, it's all crazy. How I felt that weekend, how I've felt every day since—"

"Hope, honey, we will talk about this, all of it. I promise. Okay?" he asked, ducking to capture her eyes with his. Her blue eyes were sad, and he hated it. "I missed you, too. We both did." She smiled sadly. He pressed a quick kiss to her forehead. "I have to go check on my kitchen, Hope. Don't leave, okay? Promise me."

She nodded and he sighed. He was loathe to leave her, terrified she would be gone when he returned. But he still had a kitchen to run, so this reunion would have to wait.

And he had a bone to pick with one Grant Price.

Chapter Eleven

S he was somewhere in the building. It was like a brand new
sixth sense he had. He just *knew* she was close.

Stalking around the restaurant, he table touched,
chatted with customers, small talked... all the while being
completely distracted by the fact that Hope, his Hope, was close
enough to touch. To smell. To hold. To look into those blue eyes
that he'd dreamed about damn near every night since Chicago.

And it just made him so damn angry.

Irrationally, relentlessly furious. How *dare* she show up, in *his*
fucking restaurant of all places? After sneaking out and leaving
them with *nothing*. No last name. No hint of where she lived, what
she did for a living. No way to try and find her again. Had she not
felt everything he had that weekend? That he knew Van had, too?

They didn't talk about Chicago, or Hope. They just didn't.
But he'd known that weekend changed something for both of
them. He'd thought Hope did, too... *You can't fake that kind of
connection, right?* He'd known the very first time she lied to him,
sitting in that hotel bar, about meeting her sister. She hadn't lied or
faked the entire weekend after that. He would have sensed it. A
rather annoying gift he'd always had at sensing duplicity.

So why had she left? What had been so fucking bad about the weekend that she had snuck out in the middle of the goddamn night without a single word? Why hadn't she waited until morning, so they could try and convince her to share contact information, convince her to... to what? *Stay?*

He had no idea where she lived. What kind of job she had. Hell, she could live clear across the globe for all he knew... She could just be here for a vacation, for fucks sake. Petoskey was regaled by the Smithsonian as one of the best and most popular small-towns to visit in America. Especially during peak fall color season. He knew the statistics. It was his damn job to know the statistics. She could be gone in a week, at most.

But she was here with the regular Friday night gals... his mind reminded him. He knew most of them by name, they came in often enough. So if she knew at least one of them, that meant she could be from the area, right?

Angry all over again over the painful hope that had bloomed in his chest at the idea that she could be here indefinitely, he stalked around the restaurant. The kitchen door swung open and he saw Van's back as he stood at the expo window. She was somewhere in the restaurant... alone.

Probably already running away, he thought darkly. He'd be damned before he sought her out, though. He needed time to cool off. Possibly a lot of time.

Van walked out of the kitchen and beelined for him. Glancing around the rapidly emptying restaurant, he said, "The kitchen is set for the night. We've got less than an hour before we're closed for dinner service. I'm taking her home."

Grant's hands closed into fists at his sides. "Home where?"

Van shoved his fingers up through his blonde hair, pushing it off his forehead as he glanced around. "I don't know."

"I don't want her at the condo," Grant muttered through clenched teeth. In the restaurant was bad enough... but at their *home*...

"Well I do," Van snapped back, raising his eyes to glare at him. "Dammit, Grant. I'm not letting her slip through my fingers again. Just because you're a grumpy jackass—"

"She left us. Plain and simple," Grant whispered, barely containing the rage that simmered beneath the surface. "So now we're just supposed to welcome her back with open arms—"

"Why can't we at least talk things out? Get her side of the story, figure out what happened to make her run—" Van muttered low. They were far enough away from customers and other staff, but if they raised their voices enough this conversation wasn't going to remain private. Grant grumbled under his breath and shoved his hands into his pockets. "She missed us—"

"Shut up," Grant bit out through teeth clenched so tightly together his jaw ached. The glare he was giving Van would have made any other person quail, but not his best friend. "I don't want to fucking hear anything she has to say."

"Why? You stubborn motherfucker," Van muttered, then shook his head and raised his eyes to stare at the ceiling, and Grant could tell he was counting to ten in his head in an attempt to cool his own temper. "You better figure this shit out, Grant. Because she's here and I'm not letting her walk away again. You can come around or—"

"Or what?" Grant snarled, taking a step closer. "You'll let some one-night stand come between years of friendship?"

Van's jaw ticked and the fury rolling off of him made Grant happy. Finally Van was feeling the same rage he'd been fighting since he'd seen her sitting at that table earlier. Jabbing one finger into his chest, Van bit out, "You know it wasn't just that; you're just too much of a fucking coward to admit it to yourself. You fell for her, just like I did, in next to no time at all. And that scares the living hell out of you, after everything... Well, it's not going to stop me from fighting like hell to keep her. You can come around or get the hell out of my way. You might be too scared to live after getting a second chance, but I'm not stupid enough to let her go again."

Grant's head snapped back as though he'd been physically struck, and then ice settled around him; his heart, his mind, everything. They didn't talk about that... it was an unspoken agreement. And for Van to toss it into an argument... over a woman...

"We're done here," Grant said, his voice low and deadly calm. *This... this was a low blow.*

Van backed away; his own face unreadable. "Yeah, we are. Fucking figure your shit out, Grant. She's not going anywhere."

Chapter Twelve

Van came back for her, simply taking her hand and pulling her out of the chair she'd camped herself in while he'd been gone. He had taken off his chef coat, a simple white, long-sleeved Henley in its place. He held her against him for a long time, just standing there in the center of the room. They didn't talk, just stood there in the silence of the room, wrapped around each other like two lifelines clinging together.

He finally pulled back, reaching up and tucking a strand of her hair behind her ear, before offering her his hand and leading her from the office and out the same back entrance they'd came in earlier. He led her to a sleek Lexus parked behind the restaurant, holding the passenger door open for her and letting her climb inside before rounding the hood and sliding in behind the wheel.

There was no discussion of where they were going and he didn't ask her where she was staying, but he began to drive away from the restaurant. Nervousness made her belly do flipflops.

They drove in silence, her hands clasped in his right one where it rested in her lap. His thumb stroked the back of one of her hands idly, and each pass of his skin against hers made electricity zip up her arm and straight to the center of her. She watched him as he drove out of the corner of her eye, his left hand draped loosely over the wheel. Ten minutes later, he pulled the car up to a gated entrance. He flashed a card at the reader, which buzzed lightly before the gate slowly swung open and he pulled the vehicle through. Several condominium buildings stood along the edge of Lake Michigan, and he drove them through the quiet darkness of the parking lot before stopping in front of one. He reached up and tapped a remote garage door opener and they waited while the garage door lifted.

Her heart was hammering in her chest with each passing second. She had no idea what she was doing here. Other than the fact that she was possibly still in shock from finding them... Here, in her hometown of all places. What a world.

After putting the car in park and turning off the engine, Van turned in his seat just enough to look at her through the dim interior. "I want you to know I didn't bring you here expecting anything more than conversation, Hope. Nothing more than just sitting and talking with you, little one. I need you to know that. This isn't Chicago."

She nodded, staring at him. She ran her fingers over the back of his hand, where it still clutched both of hers. "Okay."

"Wait for me," he said, nodding toward the passenger door. He opened his door and climbed out, rounding the car to hers. He opened her door, reaching in and grasping her hand again as he assisted her out. "Welcome to our home."

"Our home?" Hope whispered, sudden panic flaring in her chest. *Oh god, he's married. He's married and I'm a dirty mistress that he's sneaking into his house...*

He led her toward a door in the garage and nodded. "Grant and I split this condo."

Oh. "You and Grant?" she whispered.

"Mmhmm. We work pretty crazy hours, it just made more sense to save on a payment than for both of us to live separately, especially since we're hardly ever home. And we get along pretty well, most of the time."

"So you aren't...?"

Van opened the door and walked her through it into a wide, tiled hallway. It was dark inside except for a dim light that shined on the far end of the hallway. "Aren't what, little one?"

Her hand still held securely in his, he walked them through the hallway and it opened up into a vaulted ceilinged living room. A massive, expensive looking kitchen was situated on the right, and the light that she'd seen was from the light over the sink. Just light enough to see without running into anything, but dim enough to feel incredibly intimate. She shivered.

"Are you married?"

Van laughed, his white teeth showing up against his tanned face. He shook his head, and that blonde hair flopped over his forehead. She ached to reach up and push it back with her fingers. "Married to my job, maybe. But no, neither Grant or I are married, Hope. Nor are we involved with any other women currently."

"And you're not... involved with each other?" she asked, stopping on one side of the large marble topped island in the center of the kitchen. Everything was lavish, but surprisingly stark. As if it was more for show than for living.

Van crossed to a wide, stainless steel, double door refrigerator, opening the right side and fishing out a bottle of water and some kind of craft beer in a glass bottle. He opened the water and passed it to her before opening the beer and taking a long drink himself. He leaned his hips against the opposite counter. She fidgeted with the crinkly plastic label on the water bottle.

"No, Hope. Grant and I are not nor have we ever been involved. We told you the truth that weekend. We're business partners and roommates. We share women...on occasion. But we're not sexually or romantically involved beyond intermittent sharing. It's not like that for us."

She swallowed hard and nodded. "How did you two—"

79

Van set the beer down on the counter and crossed his arms over his chest, leveling her with an intense stare. "Do you really want to know how Grant and I started sharing women, Hope?"

"I guess not," she whispered, lowering her eyes to the floor. Porcelain faux wood tiles. Pristine white grout lines. So different than her sister's apartment, so different from her own, back in Ohio. Everything in this condo was expensive. She picked at the label on the water bottle again. "I just thought maybe it might help me understand..."

Pushing away from the counter, Van stepped toward her, slowly, cautiously, and it made her heartrate ratchet up several beats. He stopped in front of her and raised his hands to her cheeks, pushing her hair back away from her face, brushing it back over her shoulders. His hands returned to cup her cheeks, those emerald-green eyes she couldn't stop thinking about gazing into her own. "The only thing you need to understand is that it's never been like that before, Hope. Never. For myself... or Grant. He's a surly, grouchy beast right now, and I'm praying he doesn't let his pride get in the way. I won't go into details because it's his story to tell...but be patient with him. And I need you to know that I have no intention of losing you again. That weekend changed me, Hope. At the very core of me, it changed me. It changed us. We have never wanted to share for more than just a night... and we don't share girlfriends, period. That's not how we play. But with you... we were both ready to change the game."

His thumbs stroked along her cheeks, one pad of a thumb drifting over the curve of her bottom lip. Electricity zinged through her at the contact, making her lips pop open with a gasp. His eyes dropped to her mouth, then slowly climbed back up to hers. So many emotions flickered in those green depths. Joy. Fear. Sadness. Anger. Hunger.

"And then we woke up and you were gone."

Tears stung her nose again. Reaching up, she covered the backs of his hands with her palms where he was still cupping her cheeks. "Van..."

"Don't," he said gently, quietly. "Don't beat yourself up, little one. There was no way any of us could know what kind of impact that weekend would have on us at the time." Leaning his forehead against hers, she watched as he closed his eyes and rolled his forehead across hers again and again, their mouths nearly touching with each pass. "We can't change what happened or how it happened or go back and erase the last six weeks. But I need you to know that I meant it when we said in Chicago that you're ours. Ours, Hope."

The emotion fraught words that poured from him were her undoing. Nothing made sense and all of it made sense all at the same time. They could figure this out, right? Because the thought of leaving them again was not only painful, but it threatened to kill her, slowly, agonizingly. Little by little until nothing was left of her save a shell of who she was before... before them.

"Will you stay with me, please?" he asked, still clutching her cheeks between his hands. He pressed a soft kiss to the corner of her mouth, not quite on her lips, and her mouth opened in a gasp as heat spread through her entire being. The sincerity and longing in his voice nearly brought her to her knees. "Nothing has to happen, little one. I just... don't want to let you go, yet."

She nodded, brushing her lips across his. Breathing together. So close... touching, but not quite. "I don't want to let go yet, either. But, Van..."

"Yes, little one?" he breathed, angling his head, his mouth settling against the corner of her mouth.

"I don't want you to think that I don't want to..." she whispered, her words choppy. She was struggling to concentrate with him so close, with his mouth nearly on hers. She could almost taste him. She bit her bottom lip. "I just... I want to wait. For Grant, too, I mean..."

She felt Van smile against the corner of her mouth and she

sighed, a tightness in her chest easing that she hadn't realized was making it so incredibly difficult to breathe. "We'll wait for him, little one." The hands on either side of her face tightened slightly, tilting her face up closer to his as he breathed directly against her lips, "I'm not, however, going to wait to taste you."

She nodded as much as she could against the vise of his hands bracketing her jaw, and she moaned when his mouth settled on hers firmly. One of his hands fell away, and then his arm was wrapped around her lower back, hauling her closer against him. The fingers of his other hand gripped her jaw and turned her head as he leaned the opposite way, sending his tongue between her lips and tangling with hers. *Finally*.

Hope clutched at him—wanting, needing—to be closer. Pressed fully against him, they kissed and kissed until they were both breathless. Wetness pooled between her thighs and she ached from wanting him. Van shifted, stepping back just enough to slide his hand between their bodies, his hand dipping low to glide between her thighs, cupping her sex and making her knees nearly buckle.

"Fuck I can feel how wet you are through your jeans," Van panted against her lips, dragging his mouth along her jaw and up to her temple. She gasped when his fingers moved against the seam of her jeans, right where she wanted to feel him the most, her thick thighs clenching around his hand. He chuckled against her hair and dipped his head to capture her mouth with his again. Fierce, brutal. Slow, gentle. He changed tempos constantly, keeping her guessing as to what was coming next. "I can't tell you how often I dream of you, Hope. Of this. Feeling you. Tasting you. Wanting you."

"I never stop thinking about you," she whispered on a breathy sigh as his mouth dragged down her throat. Her head dropped back and she squeezed her eyes shut when his mouth settled on the curve of one breast. "I never should have left that morning."

"I don't want to talk about that right now," he murmured

throatily, palming her ass in the hand that wasn't still between her thighs, making all rational thought processes nearly impossible. "I want to be in this moment, Hope. I just want to feel you. Fuck. I missed you. I'm not too proud to say it and I don't care how crazy it sounds."

"I missed you, too," she breathed, sinking both hands into his boyishly long hair and gripping tight. His mouth was dragging across the fabric of her top, searching, and she moaned when he found his target; her nipple through her bra and material of her shirt. Electricity zinged from the place of contact all the way down to her core. He swore and tugged the neckline of her shirt down, revealing her sheer lace bra that did little to cover her. He returned his mouth to her nipple, flicking through the lacy material, making her back arch. "Oh, fuck. *Van*."

"Say it again," he mumbled around her breast, never removing his mouth from her nipple.

"Van," she breathed reverently, sliding her fingers through his hair again, pushing it from his forehead. She stared down at him, watched as his mouth laved her nipple over and over again. "Van."

"Hope," he groaned gutturally, popping his mouth off of her nipple and straightening to his full height again, taking her mouth with his in a brutal, ferocious kiss. She could feel him, heavy and hard, against her middle, and she ground into him, making him growl into her mouth. "Be good, Hope. I promised we would wait, but if you keep rubbing against me like that—"

Dropping her hand between them, she closed her fingers around the hardness behind his fly and he made a garbled sound in the back of his throat, even as his hips bucked into her hand. She smiled against his lips, nipping his lower lip gently with her teeth, which made him growl darkly. Her face was bracketed with his palms again, forcing her mouth back to his in a punishing kiss as she continued to stroke him through his pants.

"You are the devil incarnate," he groaned, tearing his mouth from hers, a grin tugging at one corner of his mouth. "Pure evil, little one."

"I am not," she whispered sullenly, tugging at the waistband of his pants. He caught her hand with his to stop her. "Van..."

"Hope, if you touch me right now, I'm not going to be able to stop until I'm buried inside you," he warned gruffly, his emerald green eyes luminous as he stared down at her. "I want you so badly, I feel like I've been dreaming about this moment for an entire lifetime... And I promised we will wait. But I'm no saint, and if you touch me, my good intentions will go straight to hell."

"*Oh*," she breathed, her mouth forming the nearly silent exclamation.

"When I'm inside you again, little one, I want to be able to go slow. I want to savor every single second in a way that we didn't in Chicago," he murmured softly, his eyes still searching hers. "We get a second chance and I'm not going to rush this time, Hope. I want to take my time like I have the rest of my lifetime to do so."

"Van..." she whimpered, tears stinging her nose at his impassioned words. *Fucking swoon*.

Her libido was rioting, of course. She had waited nearly two months to find them... hadn't had sex since Chicago and even her trusty vibrator wasn't doing the trick lately. She had a rock-hard Van pressed up against her and a promise of multiple orgasms... and her dumb mouth had opened up and said 'I want to wait for Grant'. *Face palm. Nice going, Hope.*

He pecked a kiss to her mouth. "Come to bed with me?"

"Do you really think sleeping in the same bed is a good idea?" she asked dryly as he stepped back, closing her hand in his large one.

"Absolutely not even a little bit," he laughed lightly, leading her through the living room to the other side to a short hallway. "I'll give you the formal tour tomorrow, but this is my floor of the condo." He pointed back out into the living room. "There's a bathroom back down the entry hallway, but I have an ensuite in my room as well. My office is down there—" he said and pointed toward the left side of the hall. He pushed open a door and stepped inside, flipping a light switch on that cast the room in a soft glow from two lamps suspended from the ceiling on either side of the king-sized bed set against the far wall. Wide windows looked out over the bay, dark and calm, just a hint of moonlight reflecting off the surface of the water. The room was lavish but sedately decorated in varying shades of gray and black. A dark, hunter green wall was the only color in the room, the wall and massive bed being the focal point of the room. Thick, luxurious carpet squished beneath her bare toes and she wiggled them against the softness.

"Where does Grant sleep?" she asked, glancing back out the bedroom door before he closed it behind them.

"Grant has the second floor," he said, nodding toward the ceiling. "I'd be surprised if he even comes home tonight, to be honest."

"Does he do that often?" she asked, crossing the lush carpet to sit on the edge of the comfiest bed she'd ever encountered. She spread her hands wide on the soft, thick comforter.

Van cleared his throat and shoved his hands into his pockets. He shrugged. "Sometimes. When he's had a bad week. Again, part of his story that he should be the one to tell, if and when he's ready to."

"Is it bad?" she whispered, her brows going up in worry.

Van sighed and lifted one corner of his mouth in a wry smile. "Not bad. He has next to no vices other than a taste for expensive bourbon and unlike myself, hasn't smoked a day in his life."

"You smoke?" she asked. She was learning a lot about him. Shocker.

He nodded ruefully. "A bad habit I picked up in high school and haven't been able to kick."

Hope kicked her legs, swinging them out in front of her where they dangled off the side of the bed. He had crossed the room to a large walk-in closet and flipped a light on inside. Disappearing for a minute, he came back with a neatly folded pile of clothes; a pair of navy-blue sweatpants and an oversized t-shirt. He handed them to her and she thanked him shyly, her face heating. "You know, maybe it's because I binge watched Hell's Kitchen... but I somehow expected you to be... I don't know. Scarier. Meaner. Yellier."

"Yellier?" he repeated, laughing out loud. "I don't think that's a word, Hope."

She shrugged, grinning. "It fits the situation. I think it should stand. As a chef, I just assumed you'd be yellier."

"I'll allow it just because you're cute," he chuckled, reaching up with one hand and pulling at the collar of his shirt at the back of his neck, pulling it up and over his head in one smooth motion. Hope's mouth dropped open. She'd forgotten just how ripped he was. Tall, thin, and lithe like a basketball player. And covered in tattoos from his wrists all the way up to his shoulders and across his back. "Believe it or not, we're not all giant egotistical assholes who scream at our team all the time. I'm stern, but fair. I expect excellence from my team, but understand that mistakes happen. Myself included." He glanced over at her and caught her staring and she blushed. "Stop staring at me like that, Hope. My willpower has its limits, little one."

"I can't help it," she admitted breathlessly, raising her eyes from his naked torso to his heated emerald gaze. He stalked toward her, forcing her to sit straighter on the bed, before falling back onto her hands to catch herself as she leaned back. He braced his hands on the bed on either side of her hips and leaned in close, making her heart hammer in her chest. His mouth dragged over the corner of her mouth and then down, forcing her head to tilt back so he could plant kisses along her throat and across her collarbones. She was panting.

"You are going to be the death of me," he breathed into her ear as he dragged his lips back up across her skin. She moaned involuntarily. "I'm going to have to build a goddamn pillow wall between us tonight."

She laughed then at the anguish in his voice. He pecked a kiss to her mouth and then straightened. He pointed to a second door. "Bathroom is through there. Extra toothbrushes are in the bottom drawer of the vanity."

"Do you have women guests often?" she asked as she stood, the words popping out of her mouth before she could stop them.

"Do you really want me to answer that, little one?" he asked gently.

She swallowed hard. "No," she whispered.

He nodded. "I don't want to hear about any other man before me, either, Hope. Don't mistake the golden boy attitude for softness. I'm fiercely jealous and protective of what I consider mine."

"And that's what I am?" she asked, smiling despite herself. She wanted to kick her feet with glee. "Yours?"

Gathering her into his arms, he kissed her soundly. "We told you that in Chicago, Hope. You just didn't believe us, then."

"For being so jealous and possessive, you don't seem to mind sharing me with Grant," she murmured, looping her arms around his neck.

"It's never been like this before, Hope, and I don't say that lightly. We never—and I do mean never—share girlfriends. Hookups are one thing. Relationships are something else entirely. They're emotional, messy, and someone always gets their feelings hurt."

"So what's so different about me?" she asked, shaking her head and staring up at him in wonder. "Why me?"

"I think we've both been asking ourselves that same question since Chicago," he said softly, smoothing his hands down her back. His chest was still bare, pressed against her front. "Something just...clicked, I guess. We haven't really talked about it between us...but I know he feels the same. That's why he's so ornery now that you're here. Because now it's not some fantasy, some crazy what-if... you're here, you're real, and that scares the shit out of him."

She nodded slowly, processing what he'd said, when one hand slapped her ass cheek lightly and she gasped, laughing. "Hey!"

"Go change," he laughed, winking. "I'll be here waiting for you, Hope."

"Promise?" she asked, her voice wavering lightly. Memories assailed her.

"Promise," he whispered.

Chapter Thirteen

S he was gone.

He knew it before his eyes even opened.

Groaning, Van cursed himself, cursed her. A million times over.

Opening his eyes, he looked over the mound of pillows that he had strategically stacked between them in the wide bed. He'd known if he'd touched her at all in the night he'd have woken and wouldn't have stopped until he was buried inside her, until he felt her come all over his cock, and then he would have filled her up with nearly two months of blue-balls worth of cum.

But the side of the bed that he had tucked her into was empty. The pillow still had the imprint of her head where she'd lay throughout the night. They had compromised and held hands overtop the mound of pillows, and it had been enough. His cock had protested wildly, but his heart had been content.

He sat up and scrubbed at his face, then pushed his hair off his forehead. Fucking Christ. The woman was like Houdini.

Throwing the comforter off his legs, he stood, padding across the room in the basketball shorts he'd worn to bed and nothing else. When he opened the bedroom door, the smell of fresh coffee surprised him, and then he rounded the corner to the living room. He stopped in his tracks.

Because there she was, flitting around his kitchen in nothing but his oversized t-shirt that she'd worn to bed, her blonde hair piled high on her head in an adorably messy bun. A cup of coffee was cradled between her palms and when she turned, she saw him from where he stood. She smiled brilliantly, her cheeks turning a sweet shade of pink. He leaned his shoulder against the wall and grinned over at her as he crossed his arms over his chest.

"I have to admit that I very much like the way you look in my kitchen, little one," he murmured thickly and she blushed again.

"I hope you don't mind, I woke early and was dying for some coffee," she murmured shyly, gesturing toward the coffee maker.

"No, please, make yourself at home," he said, crossing the room slowly. "I meant it when I said I like the sight of you in my kitchen. Very much so."

"You do?" she asked, tilting her head to the side as he stepped around the marble topped island that separated them. He nodded.

He was fully enjoying the way her eyes traveled over him, taking in every inch of his body that was shamelessly on display for her. He could see when her breathing changed, her lips parting slightly with each shallow, panting breath, and when the tip of her tongue darted out to wet her lips. He nearly groaned out loud as his dick hardened in his basketball shorts and felt no shame when her eyes flicked downward, taking in the growing erection there. Her eyes came back up to his, luminous and such a pretty blue in the morning sunshine that filtered in through the windows on the opposite side of the kitchen.

He reached out and took the coffee cup out of her hands, setting it on the countertop beside them before bracketing her face in his hands and tilting her face up toward his. "I thought you snuck out on me," he murmured softly, quietly. She covered his hands with her own and smiled sadly.

"I'm sorry I made you worry," she whispered earnestly, squeezing his fingers. "But I'm right here."

He stroked her cheekbone with his thumb as he stared down into those blue eyes he'd missed so much. How had one weekend changed his life so drastically?

"I want to fuck you so badly right now," he murmured huskily, a rueful chuckle escaping him. "I'm so hard, Hope."

"I can help with that," she whispered, her eyes twinkling with mischief. He groaned but shook his head, leaning down to press a quick kiss to her mouth. "Why not?"

"Because I promised we would wait, and if you touch me..."

"But I can make you come, Van. It doesn't have to be sex," she said, flicking her tongue across his lower lip. He growled down at her and she giggled.

"You naughty little thing," he growled low, nipping her lower lip with his teeth, which made her gasp into his mouth. His cock twitched at the sound and he groaned, rolling his forehead against hers. He dropped his hands from her face and grasped the fabric of the t-shirt that she was wearing, tugging it up and over her head. She raised her arms, allowing him to remove it in one fluid motion, and then he tossed it to the floor. She stood before him in nothing but a pair of purple panties, her heavy breasts just begging to be touched, kissed. He cupped them each in a hand, squeezing and kneading, before his fingers plucked at her nipples. Her back arched and she moaned on a breathy sigh, her eyelids fluttering closed. Her hands found his wrists, clutching tightly as he continued to roll her nipples between his fingers. "I want to fuck these tits, Hope. Can I?"

"Only if you let me put your cock in my mouth first," she whispered brokenly, opening her eyes dazedly. "Please."

He made a sound that was half laugh, half choke. Pinching her nipples again, he reveled in the way her body reacted to him. "You're so goddamn perfect, Hope. Such a good girl telling me

93

what you want." She nodded, her fingers clutching at his wrists still. "Get on your knees, little one."

She sank to her knees in front of him, and when she looked up at him with those big blue eyes, he was gone. He knew without a single shred of doubt that he loved her. It was certifiably insane, and he knew it, but it didn't change the fact that it was true.

She reached up and tugged the waistband of his shorts down, his impossibly hard cock springing free of the material, and then her hand was wrapped around the base, squeezing lightly. He hissed a breath in between tightly clenched teeth, wrapping his fingers around the messy topknot that her hair was tied up in and holding on for dear life. His other hand drifted over her cheek, cupping her jaw, and he growled his approval when she opened her mouth and took the head of his dick inside her mouth, then surprised the hell out of him and took him all the way to the back of her throat.

"Jesus fuck," he groaned gutturally, resisting the urge to thrust into her mouth over and over. He stared down at her as her lips closed around his cock, sucking him in, before pulling back to the tip. Her tongue laved around the head of his dick and he thought he just might explode right then. "Hope. Fucking hell, yes. Goddamn you're such a good girl."

She hummed around his cock and he growled low, fisting his hand in her hair and thrusting deep. She took it so well; this was heaven and hell on earth. She stared up at him and he'd never seen something so erotic and pretty in his entire life.

"Touch yourself," he whispered brokenly as he stared down at her. She hummed again and he groaned, clenching his jaw tight at the pleasure it caused along his shaft. Her hand disappeared between her legs, into her panties, and though he couldn't see exactly what she was doing, he could sense it. Working her fingers against her clit, he rocked his hips into her mouth. When she came around her own fingers, her moan vibrated along his dick and he felt his balls drawing up. He yanked her back, cursing wildly as her mouth popped off his dick. "Fuck, Hope. You're going to make me come just like that." She panted for breath and he leaned down, kissing her fiercely. Pulling away, he straightened, then slid his hand around the back of her neck. "Push those tits together for me, little one." She did as she was told, using her hands to push her breasts together. Widening his stance, he bent his knees slightly and then slid his cock up between her tits.

Watching his dick slide up between them, the head nearly grazing her chin as she looked down to watch, too, was his undoing. Clasping her behind the neck tightly with one hand, he covered one of her hands with his other hand, and then he was done for. Thrusting wildly, his orgasm barreled toward him quickly.

"Look at me," he growled low, his breathing ragged. She raised her eyes to his, her mouth parted with each gasping breath she took. His fingers squeezed the back of her neck and then he brought his other hand up to cup her cheek, running his thumb over her bottom lip. She ducked her head, taking his thumb into her mouth, her tongue laving the pad of his thumb as she sucked. "Fuck. Yes, Hope—"

She hummed around his thumb still in her mouth, her blue eyes luminous as she stared up at him as he came with a savage groan that built in the very pit of his being. Rope after rope of cum painted her chest and her neck, and he panted with the explosiveness of it. She released his thumb from between her lips and he stroked his fingers over her cheek as she smiled up at him. A flushed rosiness colored her cheeks and chest. He panted for breath and ducked to kiss her again thoroughly.

"Fucking hell, little one. You're perfect," he whispered against her mouth, and she grinned. He felt lighter than he had in years. Happy, hopeful, content—*and no, it wasn't the orgasm talking*. He pecked another kiss to her lips and then straightened again before tucking himself back into his shorts. "Come on. Take a shower with me?"

95

"You think that's a good idea?" she laughed, rising from the floor where she'd been kneeling. Little red marks bloomed on her knees and he very much liked the sight of it. She was such a good girl.

"I just came so hard I couldn't breathe, Hope. I need at least ten minutes to recover," he laughed and bent down to pick up the shirt he'd tossed to the floor earlier. He used it to clean up the mess he'd made across her skin, though he very much liked the way it looked. Van fought the urge to beat his chest with his fists. Caveman mode: Activated. "Besides, you're a mess."

"And who's fault is that," she teased, rolling her eyes at him. He swatted her on the ass as she turned to pick up her coffee. She gasped, turning to look at him over her shoulder, her lower lip caught between her teeth.

His dick responded, despite having just come so hard he'd seen stars. "Quit doing that or I won't be able to stop what happens next, Hope."

She laughed, shaking her head as she padded on bare feet ahead of him. Her wide hips and full bottom were too much temptation and he moved so that he could walk directly behind her, his hands settling on the curves of her waist and hips, bumping her ass with his front.

"Van..." she warned as they hurried toward his bedroom, hands fumbling as they walked.

"I won't apologize for what your body does to me," he murmured, grinning as he ducked his head, planting a kiss to the curve where her shoulder and neck met. He was already half hard again. Maybe a shower together was in fact a bad idea... But he'd never been one to have good ideas, anyway. Fuck it. Sliding his palm over one round, heavy ass cheek, he groaned, "I'll jerk off on your tits again. Or on this ass..."

She danced away into the bathroom, her throaty laughter making his heart do flipflops in his chest.

Chapter Fourteen

G rant groaned when he woke, the crick in his neck from sleeping in his office chair all night threatening to be the end of him. *Fuck I'm too old for this shit*, he thought with a grimace as he rolled his shoulders and neck, bracing his elbows on his spread knees and stretching his spine outward. He stood, groaning again, his hips screaming in agony, too. *Way too old for this shit.*

He hadn't dared go home. The knowledge that she was there, in his house, probably in Van's bed... it was too much. He was still too damn angry.

And irrationally, gut-gnawingly jealous.

He retrieved his gym bag from the corner of the room, thankful he always had an extra set of clothes. He peeled off the button-down shirt, then stripped out of the slacks and his under-wear. Pulling on a clean pair of boxer-briefs, he slid into a pair gray sweatpants before pulling a navy-blue t-shirt over his head. He rolled his neck again. The light filtering in through the window that faced the bay was weak, the sun rising on the opposite side of the building. It was early, he realized, as he checked the watch on his wrist. He found a pullover sweater in the bottom of the bag and pulled it on over his head, then pushed the sleeves up his forearms. He sighed, then repacked his gym bag with the clothes he'd worn the day before. Stuffing the black oxford shoes into the bag, he pulled out his sneakers and sat down to lace them on.

He exited his office, used the restroom, and then let himself out of the back entrance of the restaurant. They wouldn't reopen for lunch for several hours, and he was grateful that it was so early. He didn't need any employees seeing him sleeping in his office.

He tossed the gym bag into the backseat of his Audi Q8, then set out to walk the several downtown blocks to his favorite coffee shop. The mid-October morning was crisp, just chilly enough to make him glad he'd pulled the sweater on before deciding to make the walk. The leaves on the towering maples that rose above the brick buildings from the park in the middle of the downtown district were a myriad of yellows, oranges, and reds; the fall colors brilliant in the early morning sunlight that filtered over the tops of them. Shoving his hands into his pockets, he breathed in the crisp fall air, trying to alleviate some of the tension and continually roiling fury that battled inside him.

The downtown district was already bustling with the preparation of the other shops opening, and when he reached his favorite coffee shop, he pushed inside the glass door and breathed in the familiar smells of freshly brewed coffee, baked muffins, and house made soups simmering in the back. The smooth, concrete floor, red brick walls, and black ceiling, along with the heavy wood topped, black metal tables and black leather booths made the coffee shop feel homey.

He stepped forward toward the counter, where a tall, dark haired man with silver streaked throughout his hair and thick beard stood. He wore a flannel shirt left open over a black t-shirt, the sleeves of the flannel pushed up his arms, tattoos on display on his arms.

"Morning, Grant," Beau Collins called as he stepped forward. "The usual?"

"Just mine, thanks," he said, not bothering to fish his wallet out of his back pocket. One of the perks of being friends with the owner... and having done him a solid, back on Valentine's Day. Beau stepped away and poured a large cup of black coffee, bringing it back to him a moment later. "Thanks, man."

"You uh, you okay?" Beau asked, his dark brows drawing into a V. Damn man had a superpower when it came to noticing things, even the smallest details. He cleared his throat and said quietly, "It's not—"

Grant shook his head, lifting the steaming cup of coffee to his lips. He took a tentative sip. "No, it's not uh... not that. Thank you for checking in though."

Beau nodded, dropping his dark gaze to the counter where he was wiping up a spill. "That's good."

Grant nodded in return. He lifted the coffee and said a gruff, "Thanks again."

He pushed his way out the glass door back onto the sidewalk. The sun felt good as he started his way back toward the restaurant. He scrubbed a hand over his face then around to the back of his neck. He'd have to go to the condo eventually... He needed to shower, change, maybe get a power nap in before the start of another busy Saturday.

But the thought of running into Hope... no. He wasn't ready. She had been a fantasy for so long, some wild 'what if' in his mind, and now that she was here, that he was forced to realize that she was in fact real...

Waking and finding her gone that morning in Chicago had shattered a part of him that he hadn't even realized was there to break. He'd closed himself off from everyone and everything for so long... he hadn't even realized she'd slipped right under his defenses and wound her way around his damaged and steel fortressed heart.

No, if he got her alone... he would want to hurt her as deeply as she'd hurt him.

Chapter Fifteen

"This is you?" Van asked, pulling into the small driveway in front of her sister's apartment. She nodded.

"I just moved in with my sister a few days ago... I'm still looking for an apartment, but she was kind enough to let me encroach on her space until I do find something," she said. Their hands were clasped in her lap. She didn't want to let go. They'd spent the morning together, but he'd had to leave for work. He had offered to let her stay at the condo, but she'd declined, too nervous to run into Grant alone. Besides, her sister would be losing her mind, ready for details. She couldn't very well leave her to suffer.

"Can I see you again tonight?" he asked, bringing her fingers to his mouth, where his lips brushed against her knuckles.

"I'd like that," she whispered, blushing shyly. After everything that they had done... she was shocked she could still blush.

"Do you want to meet me at the restaurant at close?" he asked.

"Will Grant be there?" she murmured, raising her eyes to his. She had hoped that he would show up at the condo while she was there with Van, but he'd never shown. Van said he just needed time. "I just want to talk to him..."

"Yes, he will be there," he said and kissed her knuckles again. "I can point you in the direction of his office, let you two have a little time. I can't promise that he will be ready to talk, little one."

"I can be very persuasive," she said and grinned coyly, to which he laughed.

"That you can," he chuckled, shaking his head. His emerald green eyes were soft as he stared at her. "I don't want to let you leave."

"I promise I'm not going anywhere," she said quietly, squeezing his fingers. "I'll see you tonight?"

He nodded, then leaned over the console and kissed her, long and hard and deep. She was breathless and achy between her thighs when he finally pulled away. He grinned, reaching down to adjust himself in his pants, and she smiled against his lips.

"Fuck I can't wait to be inside you again, Hope," he whispered huskily. "This waiting is killing me, but I know it will be worth it."

She smiled, kissing him again. "Thank you."

He kissed her once more, then climbed out of the car, rounding the hood and coming to her side to open the door. He assisted her out—such a gentleman—then walked her to the front door.

"I'll see you tonight, little one," he murmured softly, grazing his fingers along her cheek, tucking a strand of her hair behind her ear. "You have my number now. Just shoot me a text when you're on your way. Feel free to sit at the bar and have a drink, I'll let Jackson or Michelle know to watch for you, and then I can come fetch you when we're done with cleanup."

She nodded, smiling up at him. He was so unfairly handsome. His blonde hair fell boyishly over his forehead, and she reached up to push it back. It was so soft against her fingertips.

He lowered his head and kissed her once more, ravenously, thoroughly. He used his entire body in his kisses, and she was quickly losing the battle against her raging libido. She needed him.

She shoved against his chest and laughed breathlessly. "Go, before I give in."

He pecked her once more on the lips and squeezed her hand. "I'll see you tonight."

He waited until she unlocked the front door and opened it, and then he was trotting down the concrete pathway toward his car, where he climbed in and waved before pulling away from the curb.

She stepped inside, greeted by Bruno, and then her sister stepped around the kitchen counter and planted both hands on her wide hips. "Umm. Okay. So I'm like, totally happy for you and not at all jealous... You know what, no, scratch that. I'm totally happy for you and a lot jealous. Because good *lawd*, Hope! That man is so fucking hot and so into you it's insane."

Hope blushed and set down her purse and a small black backpack that Van had sent home with her. The clothes she'd worn to dinner the night before were tucked inside, and she was wearing a pair of his navy sweatpants and an oversized crewneck sweatshirt that Van had rolled the sleeves up to her wrists. He'd made her wait in the car while he ran inside the local Walgreens to purchase a pair of slippers for her, just so she didn't have to wear her heels. He was incredibly sweet, and thoughtful. And hot.

Waggling her strawberry blonde eyebrows, Jade asked lasciviously, "So... did y'all..."

She blushed again, but shook her head. "No. We did not."

"Woman, I would have jumped that man like he was a trampoline," Jade muttered, shaking her head in disappointment. Hope laughed.

"Just because things were hot and heavy in Chicago doesn't mean we just jumped right back into bed now," she murmured, crossing to the refrigerator. She opened it, pulled out a bottle of water, and uncapped it before taking several long swallows. "Besides, Grant is... upset, at how I left that weekend. I want to talk to him before anything else happens. It's only fair. And..."

"And you want both of them, I get it," Jade said and nodded. This was why her sister was her favorite person. They just... got each other. No judgement. No censure. "If I could have my cake and eat it too, I would in a fucking heartbeat."

Hope sank down into a corner of the couch, her shoulders sagging. "You won't tell Mom or Dad, right? I don't want to cause a heart attack for Dad…"

Jade waved a hand dismissively as she sank into the opposite corner. "Let me share a childhood trauma with you; Mom and Dad were swingers when they were our age. Remember their best friends' Pam and Ed?" Hope's mouth fell open, and she nodded slowly. Jade raised her eyebrows and smirked. "Remember that big falling out they all had when you were like, I'd say… fourteen?" Again, Hope nodded, her brain short circuiting with the new information. "Yeah… They were all swinging together. Came home sick from a sleepover at Angie's one weekend…" she shuddered and Hope made a strangled laughing sound in the back of her throat. *Oh my gawwwd. Ewww.* "Anyway. I guess they all ended up catching feelings for each other and it got messy, so things ended, as did their friendship. Ran into Ed at a bar once, like two years ago. He was *hammered* and told me the whole thing. So much childhood trauma brought back."

"That… is so much more information than I ever needed to know about our parents," Hope whispered, staring blankly ahead of her. Jade slapped her thigh and laughed.

"You're welcome," Jade chortled as she pushed herself up from the couch. "I'm on my way to the gym, I'll see you later?"

Hope nodded, then waved as her sister picked up a gym bag and headed out the door. Bruno padded over to her, resting his white muzzled chin on her knee. She ruffled his ears and bent low to whisper, "Your Mom just scarred me for life. She's evil."

His floofy tail swished behind him in a slow wag. She smiled and pressed a kiss to his white face.

Chapter Sixteen

Her heart in her throat, she sent the text message to Van, letting him know she was sitting at the bar at The Wine Garden. The restaurant was nearly empty, the dinner evening winding down. Only a few people remained at the other end of the polished bar, all of which looked like employees counting workbooks of cash or polishing a bin of silverware. She sat in one of the swiveling barstools as a gentleman with dark, flawless skin and short cropped black hair stepped over to her. He wore black button-down shirt and black slacks, and his white teeth shone brightly in his dark face.

"Hello, miss. What can I get for you?" he asked above the soft instrumental music that played throughout the restaurant.

"Oh, umm," she said, glancing behind him at the row of liquor and wine bottles. Returning her gaze to his, she smiled and said, "May I please get a glass of Cabernet? Doesn't matter what kind. I'm just waiting for—"

"Chef?" he asked with a smile, motioning toward the kitchen with his head, and she laughed, nodding. "He said to expect you. Hope, I assume? I'm Jackson."

"Yes," she said and smiled again. He nodded and turned to

pour her wine, bringing it back to her a moment later. She pulled her purse into her lap, but he waved her off when she attempted to slide him her card.

"Chef made it clear that whatever you want is on the house," he said and grinned.

Her phone buzzed inside her purse where it was still sitting in her lap. She slipped it out and smiled when she saw Van's name on her screen, along with the photo of the two of them he'd insisted they take earlier in the day. She had repeatedly opened her phone to the photo library throughout the evening, swiping through the collection of selfies they'd taken together. She never wanted to stop looking at his stupidly handsome face. Swiping open the phone, she read:

> Van: I should be set in just a few more minutes.
> I'll see you soon, little one.

She smiled and sent back:

> Hope: You didn't have to comp my drink. I can
> pay for it myself.

She had barely set her phone down on the polished bar when it buzzed. Picking it back up, she rolled her eyes when she read his text.

> Van: Say 'Thank you, Chef'.

She typed back, blushing furiously:

> Hope: Thank you, Chef.

Immediately, the three dots popped up on the bottom of the screen, and then:

Van: Good girl. I won't be long. No flirting with
my bartender.

Hope choked on the swallow of wine she just took. The bartender in question stepped over to her, his dark brows drawing together in concern. "Are you alright?"

She nodded, wheezing, as she set her glass down. "Yes, I'm sorry. Wrong tube."

Swiping through the photos again and sipping the wine, she was surprised when ten minutes had passed and her wine glass was empty in her hand. She felt bad, sitting at the bar while the employees were cleaning around her, and she set the glass on the bar so Jackson could clear it. Instead, he held up the bottle of cabernet and asked if she would like another. Glancing at the time, she then nodded. Why not.

Van swooped in over her shoulder a few minutes later, leaning over her and planting a full, thorough kiss on her lips. When he pulled away, she felt a blush spread across her cheeks, unsure if it was from his kiss or the wine she'd consumed. She bit her lip and glanced sideways at the employees that remained sitting at the far end of the bar, who had stopped talking amongst themselves and were shamelessly staring at them.

"If you're done for the evening, make sure Michelle checks you all out before you leave," Van called down the bar, and the three employees averted their gazes, fumbling with their cashbooks and the heavy bin of silverware. She blushed a darker shade of red when she heard a chorus of "Yes, Chef" come from the three of them.

"I have to bandage a slice on one of my new kids' hands and it might take a bit, do you want me to take you to Grant's office? Are you ready to talk?" he asked, leaning against the bar to her right, his right arm crossed over her body and holding onto the curve of her left hip.

"Sure," she said and nodded, her heart climbing into her

throat. Van stepped back and assisted her from her seat, making a low whistle.

"I will never get tired of looking at you," he whispered huskily, ducking his head to run his lips along the curve of her jaw. "So beautiful."

She blushed and rolled her eyes. "It's just a skirt, Van."

He held her away from him at arm's length and looked at her fully as he walked backward toward a door labeled for employees only.

She wore a pretty, dark gold/burnt umber wrap skirt in a silky, satiny material that floated around her knees with a soft ruffle along the edge and up one leg to where it tied at her waist. A simple black, cropped sweater covered her arms and chest, the hem tucked into the waist of her skirt at the front. A pair of comfortable black ballerina flats adorned her feet.

"My statement stands," he murmured low as they passed down the hallway, squeezing her hand lightly. He stopped them beside a door and nodded to it. "I just have to bandage this kid's hand. If you're not out in the restaurant when I'm done, I'll wait for you, okay? Do you need me to come in with you?"

"No," she murmured, squeezing his hand in return. "I think it'll be okay. I'll find you."

He ducked his head and kissed her soundly. "I'll be waiting. Good luck."

She rolled her eyes. "Thanks. I might need it."

He swatted her bottom playfully as he started to walk away and winked at her over his shoulder. When she heard the door at the end of the short hallway click closed, she turned toward the closed door of Grant's office. A sliver of light could be seen beneath the door. Taking a deep, courage bolstering breath in, she raised her hand and knocked.

"Come in," she heard him call gruffly through the door, and then she reached for the handle and turned it, pushing the door open. She stepped inside and closed it before raising her eyes to his where he stood on the other side of a smooth, polished wooden desk. A set of windows overlooked the bay behind him, though it was so dark outside all she could see was just a hint of waves as the moonlight reflected off of them in the distance. One dim lamp was turned on in the corner of the room, casting him half in shadow.

"Hi..." she whispered nervously, licking her lips. He was staring at her, his jaw clenched tight. When he made no move to greet her or soften his gaze, she fidgeted with her purse. "I didn't know how else to find you... I just want to talk," she said, swallowing hard. Her eyes traveled over him, but didn't linger, dropping to the floor when the anger in his eyes didn't abate. The harsh lines of his face made her chest ache. "Van showed me—"

"Van can mind his own fucking business." The words were harsh, clipped, and strained with rage. His hands were shoved into the front pockets of his slacks, and he remained where he was, standing on the other side of his desk.

She swallowed again, nodding. "I'm sorry, I—"

"Get out, Hope."

Her shoulders sagged. This was not going as well as she had hoped. Maybe she should have taken Van up on his offer to stay.

"Please let me explain—"

"I said. Get. Out." The quiet words were bitten out through tightly clenched teeth and she faltered back a step as she stared at him. "Get the fuck out of my office. Now."

Lifting her chin, she leveled him with a stare that was far more confident than she felt. "No."

His dark brows rose in surprise, but his facial expression did not soften. Pulling his hands out of his pockets, he braced them, palms flat, on the top of his desk and leaned on them. "You have ten seconds to leave before you regret it, Hope."

She shook her head.

"Ten."

"I'm not leaving."

"Nine."

"Stop. Please, Grant," she whispered.

"Eight." He straightened.

She gulped and shook her head.

"Seven."

"I'm not leaving until you talk to me!" she cried, shifting her weight from one foot to the other nervously.

"Oh, we won't be talking. Six," he growled low, rounding the corner of his desk.

She trembled where she stood. "You don't scare me, Grant."

The laugh that escaped him was hard and so devoid of emotion she almost fled. Almost. "I should scare you. Five."

"You won't hurt me," she whispered, tilting her head back to look up at him as he stepped closer.

"I plan to. Four."

Again, she shook her head. He rolled his shoulders, staring down at her.

"Three. This is your last chance, Hope."

"You won't hurt me," she repeated on a whisper, her voice quivering slightly.

"Butterfly, I'm going to hurt you as badly as you hurt me," he whispered the warning, and she shook like a leaf. "Two."

Her heart was hammering in her chest. But she wouldn't back down.

"One."

"Grant—"

His hand snapped out and his palm covered her mouth, silencing her, at the same time that his other arm banded around her waist. "No. You don't get to talk now. You had your chance to leave and you didn't take it. Now, I'm going to exorcise you out of my fucking system. However I want. Do you understand?" She nodded mutely against his hand that still covered her mouth and he growled, removing his hand. "Yes or no, Hope? I need one word."

"Yes, but, Van—"

He shushed her gruffly, shaking his head.

"Grant, I want—" she said breathlessly, trembling from head to toe when he shushed her again.

"I said you don't get to talk," he reminded her roughly, and she bit her bottom lip.

"But, Van—"

Grant growled low in his throat, the sound menacing, and it vibrated through her chest before he pushed her away roughly and spun her around so that she was facing his desk. His palm planted on the flat of her back and pushed until she was bent over the desk, her front plastered to the smooth top. Her hands came out to hold herself up, but then his hands were there, pulling them behind her. He gathered her wrists in one hand and reached up beneath her skirt to yank her panties down her legs. Oh god. Just the touch of his fingertips against her aching flesh was enough to make her pant against the smooth wooden top of the desk. Her breath fogged up the polished surface with every exhale, and she focused on calming her breaths. It was Grant, and she trusted him. If this is what he needed to exorcise the anger he was still fighting, she would be whatever he needed her to be.

"Pick a safe word," he muttered low from behind her.

"What?" she asked, her desire fogged brain not comprehending what he'd said.

"A safe word, Hope. Pick one," he snarled, and then he bent at the waist, sliding her panties down her legs until she stepped out of them, and then she gasped, because he was using her panties to tie her wrists together behind her back. Holy shit. "Now."

"Caterpillar," she gasped. "Caterpillar."

The chuckle that rumbled out of him was dark and it skittered over her rapidly fraying nerves. His fingers were back under her skirt then, pushing the material up and over her hips until her ass was bare for him. "I won't stop unless you use it. Remember that, butterfly." She nodded mutely.

His hand smoothed over the plumpness of one ass cheek, and

she sighed, wiggling just a tiny bit. Then his hand disappeared and a second later she cried out abruptly, stunned, as pain radiated from her right butt cheek. Twisting her head sharply, she looked back at him where he stood behind her, her teeth clamping down onto her lower lip from the pain.

He'd spanked her. Fucking *hard*.

His palm smoothed over the spot he'd just struck, and she scrunched up her face at the sting of it. Then his hand raised, and she braced herself a heartbeat before his palm came back down on her flesh.

He did it again and she bit her lip to keep from crying out, pressing her forehead hard to the top of the desk. Tears stung her eyes, but she refused to let them fall. As much as it hurt, heat flooded her insides. They'd played in Chicago... but not like this.

She felt him step to the side of her, so that his lap was pressed tight against her hip, just as his fingers slid down and between her legs. She felt him, hard at her hip and shifted, trying to grind against his lap. She hiccupped on a sob when his fingers slid inside her, one, then two, so deep. His body bent low over her back, his mouth at her ear as he grunted, "You like being spanked, don't you, butterfly? You're so fucking wet."

He pumped his hand, finger fucking her over his desk, finding that spot inside and flicking it deftly. She cried out, straining against the panties that bound her wrists and his weight against her back and side. She was so close—

He pulled his fingers out just as she was about to shatter, and she sobbed, her body sagging against the desk in frustration as her orgasm flitted away, just out of reach. His palm landed on her other ass cheek as he shifted away from her back.

She gasped when his fingers wrapped around the backs of her arms, hauling her up off the desk before spinning her to face him. "On your knees," he growled, and she sank to the carpeted floor. Her hands were still tied behind her back, her arms aching.

She watched as his hands went to his belt, the metallic clink of the buckle being released ringing in her ears, a second before she watched as he dragged the straining zipper down. He lowered his slacks just enough on his hips to allow his erection to spring free, still confined by the black boxer briefs that did little to hide it. He palmed himself crudely, working his hand over the bulge inside his underwear as his other hand fisted in her hair at the back of her head.

She was panting. His thumb hooked into his underwear and yanked them down, finally revealing his straining cock, a bead of precum already glistening on the tip. She licked her lips.

"Open your mouth." His voice rumbled from way above her, and she hesitated for a heartbeat. The fingers in her hair tightened and she gasped. "I said open. I'm going to fuck this mouth, and you will take it. Understood?"

She nodded. Opening her mouth wide, she stared up at him as the hand still in her hair held her still while his other hand gripped his cock and guided it into her mouth. He slid in, all the way to the back of her throat, and she gagged, tears filling her eyes, but she closed her lips around him, sucking him in.

She moaned when his other hand came up and both of his hands bracketed her head, holding her still as he pumped his hips in and out, fucking her mouth over and over again. She was so wet. She ached to touch herself, but with her hands tied behind her back, she was at his mercy. Just when she started to panic that he wasn't going to let her breathe, he slid out, patting her cheek and allowing her to suck in air before sliding back in to fuck her throat again. She was so wet; she could feel it between her tightly clenched thighs.

"Fuck," he snarled, curling her hair around his fist and pulling back sharply. His dick popped out of her mouth and she panted, shaking. He reached down and lifted her under her arms, and once again on her feet, her legs shook. His fingers gripped her chin hard, turning her face up to his, and she reached for his mouth with hers. He turned her away sharply at the last second, spinning her so that her back was to him again. She let out a whine of disappointment at being denied his mouth, his kiss, and he spanked her ass again hard, making her choke back a scream of pain. Her pussy throbbed with need. He wrapped his fingers around her throat and pressed his front tightly against her back and she shifted, grinding against him with a strangled moan. Speaking directly into her ear, he growled, "Good girls get kissed, butterfly. Do you think you deserve a kiss? I don't."

Hurt lanced through her sharply, making her chest ache and tears prick behind her eyes. This wasn't the Grant she'd met in Chicago, and she realized then that he had meant it when he said he was going to hurt her. She just hadn't expected it to hurt so deeply. Hadn't expected him to *want* to hurt her, *not really*.

Bending her forward over the desk again, she went willingly, and he kicked her feet together. As much as her heart ached inside her chest, she still wanted him. Needed to feel him. Unable to see him behind her, she closed her eyes and listened, instead. Their labored breaths were the only sounds in the small office. She heard the telltale rip of a condom wrapper being torn open. And then his massive hands were spanning her soft hips as he planted his feet wide to accommodate for his height, the broad head of his cock notched at her entrance. Panic set in. *Wait!* her mind railed. *Van! She was supposed to wait—*

"Grant, wait—" she started, but the plea was cut short when he thrust hard, seating himself all the way inside her. She moaned, the sensation of being so full of him again after so long making her head spin. He ground his hips into her from behind, the edge of the desk cutting into the notch of her thighs where she was bent over it. She turned her head, resting her flushed cheek against the coolness of the desk beneath her. She could just see him over the curve of her shoulder. Her inner walls convulsed around him where he was pressed so deep. "Oh, god."

"Fuck," he groaned behind her, and she saw his head tipped back to stare at the ceiling. His breaths sawed in and out of him, his chest heaving, and she hiccupped a sob at the raw emotion she could feel radiating off of him. His hips pumped in slow, shallow thrusts, his fingers digging into the fleshy curves of her waist. "You come back into our lives like a goddamn hurricane, making a mess of everything. You're already coming between us, butterfly, and you need to learn."

His palm cracked against the meaty part of her butt again and she rolled her cheek on the desk on another sob. Pain pierced through her chest at his words. *She wasn't trying to make a mess of anything.* He pulled out and slammed back in, just once, and she moaned, distracted by the pleasure. It was so... primal. It felt so good, and so wrong. Everything hurt, but it just felt *so good*. And she had missed him. If this was what he needed, she could do it, even if it killed her inside. *God, but Van... he'd promised, and she was—*

Twisting her head, she panted brokenly, "I'm not trying to—I won't, I promise. But Grant, please... *I need Van—*"

Pulling out all the way to the tip, he slammed back in, turning her words into another throaty moan. The edge of the desk hurt where it cut into her skin, but she didn't care. Her fingers clenched and unclenched against her back, and she wished more than anything that she could touch him. She needed to feel him. Betrayal and guilt stabbed through her and tears stung her nose. This was going to kill Van. Fuck but it felt *so good*... she had missed them, so much...

Grant pounded into her fiercely. He was far rougher than he'd been in Chicago, brutal in his intensity; his hips slapping into the backs of hers, her already stinging flesh tender from the spankings he'd doled out. He murmured from behind her; low, dark words she couldn't make out, but they sounded filthy and heady and wanton, if a touch angry, and so fraught with emotion. Her legs started to shake, and she panted against the desk. "Oh fuck, please Grant—"

But he stopped just as she was about to go over again, and she moaned in disappointment as the second orgasm he'd denied her abated. Leaning low over her back, he growled in her ear, "Whose cock is inside you, Hope? Hmm?"

"*Grant*," she moaned, tossing her head on the desk, rolling her cheek on the cool surface. Tears stung her nose again. This was supposed to be different. It was supposed to be all of them... But she whispered, "Yours."

"Yes, *mine*. Not Van's," he grunted low as he started again when all the remaining spasms had ceased, fucking her roughly until she was back at that precipice. Her heart seized in her chest. *Van.* Tears pricked her eyes, sweat was beaded on her forehead, and she could feel it down her spine under her sweater. She wanted Van —but she wanted to come so bad. *She was so close again, so close, yes!*—

Grant pulled sharply out of her, once again denying her an orgasm, and this time she sobbed as tears finally slid down her cheeks. She pressed her forehead against the desk, rolling it back and forth in agony. She knew then that he wasn't going to let her finish. This was punishment. He was angry and hurt. She had hurt him, deeper than she had realized, and he had warned her he would hurt her, too. She hadn't believed him. Hadn't believed he would hurt her *this* badly. Not like this. On purpose. And for the first time, she was glad that Van *wasn't* here for this. She had ruined it all.

Gripping her hips in his hands again, she sagged against the desk as the tears continued to slide down her cheeks. Her mind, her body, and her heart were all at war. None of them would come out the winner, though, not in this. When he went deep, she bit her lip and clenched her eyes tightly closed against the ecstasy of having him fill her so completely.

And when he came, pulsing inside her, she felt his chest heave; heard his low, throaty groan, and she hated him.

She hated that she *didn't* hate him.

Panting into the dim room around them, Grant backed away

and pulled out of her, and she bit her lip again to keep from crying out as pain started to spread through her as the adrenaline and dopamine began to abate. Her arms ached. Her wrists were sore. Her pussy was throbbing with the need to come and with how rough he'd been. Her pride was torn to shreds. Her heart... well, that lay tattered and beaten in her chest. She didn't move, just continued to lay face down on the desk, her ass and pussy still bared to him.

She felt used, and not in the good way. Not like Chicago. This was nothing like Chicago.

The panties binding her wrists were removed, and she dropped her aching arms onto the desk. Her underwear landed on the desk next to her in an unceremonious heap and she stared at them through tear clouded eyes. Shaking uncontrollably, the tears continued to track down her cheeks, but she refused to reach up to swipe them away. She wouldn't give him that satisfaction, even if it killed her. Because right now it felt like it just might.

She heard the rustling of his clothes as he tucked himself back into his pants and then the zipper as it closed. "Get the fuck out of my restaurant."

The swish of the door opening, his heavy footsteps, and then the click of the door as it closed behind him reverberated through her mind like a gunshot. Pushing herself up with shaky arms, she sucked in shuddering breaths. Reaching up, she finally swiped at the tears marring her face. He'd warned her. God, he'd warned her.

Her ass was on fire, and she was sure she would find angry red handprints later. The ones he'd left on her in Chicago had disappeared within a few hours. These... she didn't think these would go away quite so quickly. Struggling to stand on her shaking legs, she managed to pull her panties back on, then smoothed the skirt down her legs.

Using her fingers, she attempted to tame the mess he'd made of her hair, then gave up. She just prayed she wouldn't run into any remaining employees on her way out.

Pulling the door open, she glanced out and when she felt the coast was clear, snuck down the hallway to the main part of the restaurant. She didn't trust going out the back entrance, sure that either Grant or Van would be there. The central part of the building was dark, most of the lights turned off for the night. She checked the door to make sure it latched and locked on her way out. Breathing a sigh of relief when she made it outside with no one seeing her, she thanked every lucky star in the night sky as they winked above her. She needed to escape before Van found her.

Wrapping her arms around her middle, she sniffled as tears started again, the damn things. Turning up the sidewalk, she stumbled when she heard, "Hope? How'd it go?"

Her shoulders dropped and she made a quarter turn, just barely enough to see him. *No...* He was going to hate her, just like Grant did. He was leaning against one of the exterior walls of *The Wine Garden*, a cigarette glowing in his hand. When the light from the streetlight above her landed on her face, he took a step toward her, but she held up her hand and backed away.

"Wait, Hope, where are you going?" he asked in confusion, taking another step toward her.

"Please, just leave me alone," she whispered miserably. Her heart was shattered, the shards of her heart lancing through her, cutting everything inside until there was nothing left but shreds. Taking a deep breath, she cursed the tears that wouldn't stop. Gesturing toward the building, where Grant was somewhere inside, she whispered brokenly, "I'm so sorry, Van. I can't... I can't do this. I can't do that again."

"Wait, *Hope*—" he called, taking another step toward her, his face pulling into one of shock and worry.

"Please just let me go," she begged, backing away as he continued forward. If he touched her, she would break, and the mess her heart had made inside would spill out of her. Her chest ached, as if her heart had been pulled from her body and set on fire, then trampled. Van flicked the cigarette down to the pavement and stepped on it, striding toward her. Still, she backed away, up the gently sloping sidewalk. He caught up to her, bracketing her face in his hands. He tilted her face up so she was forced to look at him and she tried to shake her head. "Please, Van. Just let me go."

"*What happened?*" he demanded with a growl, his eyes roving over her tear-streaked face, the tangled mess of her hair. She knew one spot on her cheek had to be red, where she'd had it pressed to the hard desk.

She hiccupped and shook her head. "I'm so sorry. I didn't mean for it to happen—" She shook her head again, damning the tears that wouldn't stop. God, he was going to hate her. And Grant was right; coming home, coming here, she had only made things worse. So much worse. This whole thing should have stayed in Chicago. Her chest threatened to cleave in two. "I made a mistake c-coming here. Coming h-home. I made a mess of everything—"

"*Don't you dare talk like that,*" he gritted out, searching her eyes with his. "Don't you dare talk like that, Hope. You're ours. You belong here, with us."

"He h-hates me," she sobbed and shook her head, gripping his fingers where they were clasped at her cheeks. His thumbs stroked over her skin, swiping the tears away. "And now you will, too. I can't—I can't do this, Van."

"Why on earth would I hate you?" Van murmured, his words soft but intense, his green eyes boring into hers. The emotion in them... it was breaking her. What was left of her, anyway. "I'm not losing you again. I will not let you walk away from me again, Hope. I can't. He'll come around—"

But Hope shook her head, her lip wobbling. "He won't, Van."

"No," Van bit out, his fingers tightening around her face, and she swallowed another sob. "No, Hope. You're not running again. *I need you.*"

"I need you, too," she whispered sadly. "But I won't come

between you and Grant. I won't choose... and I won't let you, either."

"*No,*" he ground out through clenched teeth. "No. Do you hear me? You're not running from us, Hope. You belong to *both of us.*"

"I wish that were the truth," she whispered, leaning her cheek into one of his hands. "I think we need to accept that what happened in Chicago was just a crazy, amazing, wild weekend... and that maybe that's how it should stay."

"No, Hope," he argued, pressing his forehead to hers. "Please. Don't do this. Don't leave me."

She laughed softly, sadly. Squeezing his fingers that still cupped her cheeks, she whispered, "I couldn't choose between you in Chicago... What makes you think I could do it now, knowing I'm falling in love with both of you?"

"*Hope,*" he groaned, squeezing his eyes shut, and she couldn't stop the sob that escaped her. He was breaking her heart. Well, what part of it wasn't already broken by Grant. "Please don't do this. *I love you.*"

Another sob broke free of her throat and she shook her head, fighting every fiber of her being from saying those words back to him. Not now. She needed him to let her go. "He's never going to forgive me, and you won't either... and I can't do... whatever that was. Not again."

"What happened?" he demanded again, staring at her. His gaze traveled over her then, as if assessing for any injuries. "*What happened,* Hope? What did he do? Did he hurt you?"

"We—he... he was so mad— and he..." She hiccupped, shaking her head miserably. "I'm sorry."

"Wait... did he..." Rage crossed his features and she felt him trembling. "Did he force you?"

She shook her head again miserably, her lower lip wobbling uncontrollably. "No. No, Van. He just wasn't listening when I tried to tell him—"

"That you wanted to wait," he finished on a whisper, squeezing his eyes shut. He pressed his forehead to hers, his hands clasped tightly around her face. "Fuck, Hope. I'm sorry."

"I can't do this, Van," she sobbed, clutching his hands where they bracketed her face. "I already love you both so much, and I hate that this is how it has to be. But I can't do that again."

"No, god dammit!" Van ground out through clenched teeth. Tears tracked down her cheeks and he swiped at them gently. "No. I'm not letting you walk away. *I can't.*"

She smiled sadly, her lower lip wobbling. "You have to. Please."

"I can't," he ground out. "I won't, Hope."

"Please don't make this harder than it already is," she begged, trying to pull away from him. He released her face, but encircled her with his arms, drawing her so close to his body there was no way to tell them apart. He rocked her in his arms as she clutched at him, never wanting to let go but knowing it was inevitable. This was never meant to work. And she had just made it worse. They would have been fine if she'd never come back home, never walked into their restaurant. One of his hands pressed her face into the crook of his neck, curving his body around hers as she cried. "Please, Van."

"I will give you time, Hope, but I will not let you run away from me again," he whispered into her hair, and her heart broke when she heard the raw emotion in his voice making his words rough. "Do you hear me? You are ours, even if that stupid bastard is too cowardly to see it right now. You don't get to run away. Never again."

She nodded, wanting to believe his words more than anything in the world. But he hadn't seen the fury in Grant, hadn't heard the pain in his words. And she couldn't stand to be witness to what would happen between the two friends if she stayed.

Chapter Seventeen

The punch that landed on his cheekbone, just below his left eye, was well deserved. As was the second one.

When Van swung at him a third time, though, he caught his friend's hand and stopped him, shoving him away. Van growled and dropped his head, ramming into his chest hard enough to seize his breath. Grant wrapped his arms around Van's middle, picking him up off the ground and tossing him away.

"You bastard," Van shouted as he regained his footing, and Grant just nodded. "*What did you do?* She's fucking *leaving*, Grant! She said she's falling in love with us, and she's leaving! She said if she can't have both of us, she doesn't want either of us. So, she's fucking leaving me, too. *We just fucking found her!*"

Stalking away, Van shoved his fingers through his hair, his chest heaving. Grant just stared at his friend.

"God dammit, you emotionally stunted son of a bitch!" Van raged, coming back at him. Pointing toward the exterior of the building, he shouted, "She just left here sobbing, Grant. She looked so goddamn broken. What the fuck did you do?!"

"Do you see what's happening?" Grant asked gruffly, shoving his hands into his pockets and turning away.

"I see a woman that is somehow crazy about both of us —*somehow loves both of us*—running scared because you're a jackass," Van muttered, shaking his head. Grant swallowed hard. She couldn't. She wouldn't, not now, anyway. His own actions would make sure of that. He'd seen the tears tracking down her cheeks as she lay motionless against the desk. It had gutted him. Fuck, everything about her gutted him. Being around her, not being around her. Grant grunted when Van shoved his shoulder, spinning him back to face him. "What did you do to her?"

"I did what I told her I would," he muttered. Guilt gnawed at his gut, making his stomach heave. He had hurt her. Deeply.

"You fucked her like you hate her," Van snapped, shaking his head again in disbelief, calling him out. Fucker knew him too well. "Well, congratulations. Because she fucking believes it."

"Like you haven't fucked her again since we found her?" Grant deflected, muttering with a disdainful snort as he glared at his friend.

Van took a deep breath in and let it out just as slowly before turning and walking to the door. He stopped there, turning before he exited and said quietly, "No, actually, we haven't had sex. She wanted to wait for you. She wanted it to be all of us again. So, yeah... Thanks for that."

And then Van walked out of the office and down the hall, and the pleaded words she'd tried to convey to him came back to him. She had tried to tell him, and he hadn't listened. Had been so convinced that she and Van had already... and his jealousy and rage had been too volatile, his ego too fragile to be willing to listen to her quiet pleas.

Fuck he'd made a mess of things. He'd been so damn angry, so hurt... he'd wanted her to know how it felt. Just how deeply she'd cut him to pieces when she left. Not that any of it made any rational sense. He had no right to be this fucking angry... but knowing that didn't stop it from boiling out of him like a poisonous sludge. His rage was infecting everything around him, including Hope. Now he'd hurt his best friend, too. *Fucking hell.*

She'd let him treat her terribly. Used her, then tossed her aside like the condom he'd taken off and buried in the trash in the men's restroom. When all he'd wanted to do was hold her, kiss her, make love to her. Slowly, passionately, tenderly. Reminding her just how safe she was with them, with him. But all he'd done is show her how much of a sorry excuse for a bastard he was instead.

Ten years was a long time to avoid emotional attachments. Ten years and a medical diagnosis that had turned his world upside down... until the moment he'd met her and everything had felt right again. For the first time in a decade, he'd been able to see a future, and not just next week, or beyond the next doctor's appointment...

Most men didn't get a prostate cancer diagnosis at the age of thirty-two. Despite the early diagnosis, rapid fire treatment, and nearly seven years of remission...he often wondered if he would ever feel normal again. Or if it would come back.

Hope had made him feel normal. *Hopeful.* Something had settled inside him, that constant anxiety that seemed to just live inside his chest at all times had quieted. For the first time in a decade, he'd wanted to wake up with her at his side every single morning, for whatever foreseeable future he was being granted. She could be his second chance in more ways than one.

And Van was right; it scared the living hell out of him.

Being vulnerable opened you up to too much pain. Too much heartache. She would leave once she knew the truth. All of his dark secrets. The unpredictability of the future. Just like Nicole had.

Grinding his teeth together, he shoved the thought away, but it was too late. Like a dam bursting open, those long-repressed memories resurfaced and threatened to drown him.

Chapter Eighteen

H e was staring at his cellphone screen, willing a text to come through from Hope as he lay in bed, his right hand on his chest, a bag of frozen peas balanced on the back of it. He hadn't bothered with bandaging his busted knuckles the night before, not that he'd come home. He'd slept in his car, outside of Hope's sister's house, just in case she needed him. Just in case she messaged and wanted him to come to her. Just in case...

But she hadn't messaged, last night or this morning. Jade had come outside, wearing a matching set of sweatpants and cropped, zippered hoodie, her arms crossed over her chest. It was drizzling, cold and gloomy. She waited until he climbed out of the car, hunching her shoulders against the chill as it soaked her clothes.

"Van... you need to go home," she said, softly, gently. Her eyes were kind, but he could tell by the tightness of her face that she was over the bullshit. He could only imagine the state Hope had been in when she got home the night before, and didn't blame her sister one bit for not wanting him there. "She cried all night. She won't tell me what happened, but I can tell... Van, whatever happened, it broke her. She just needs time, okay?"

He wanted to protest. Wanted to tell her *No, she needed* him. *Not time. No, time... time was what she needed to* run. *And that wasn't happening again.*

"Just... tell her I was here, okay? Tell her I'm not giving up," he whispered, glancing across the street at the small house. "I just found her, Jade... I can't lose her again already."

She had nodded, giving him a wilted smile, before she turned and hurried back across the road in the rain, disappearing into the house. He had finally driven home, not at all surprised to not find Grant's car in the garage... so despite the early hour, he'd raided Grant's bourbon.

Now, several hours later, a large glass of Grant's favorite bourbon was sitting on the bedside table next to him. It was the third time he'd refilled it. Tossing the phone onto the mattress, he picked up the bourbon and took several long swallows of the amber liquid, relishing the burn as it went down. He was pleasantly drunk, but it did little to ease the ache in his chest.

The sound of the front door opening and closing alerted him to Grant's arrival home. Heavy footsteps echoed through the empty condo, reminding him of just how empty their home was. More so now that he had gotten to experience Hope in it with him. He hated it without her.

A knock sounded on the bedroom door, though it wasn't shut all the way. It swung open and Grant leaned his shoulder against the doorframe, hands shoved deeply into the pockets of his slacks.

"I realize I fucked up."

"No shit," Van mumbled, tossing back another swallow of the bourbon. The discoloration under Grant's left eye gave him a perverse sense of pleasure. He flexed his fingers beneath the bag of peas, the frozen vegetables settling in the bag again with an audible swoosh. He dropped his eyes, not able to keep looking at him through his anger. "You're brilliant if you came up with that all on your own."

The sarcasm in his voice was punctuated with the slight slur of his words from the alcohol. Grant sighed, pulling one hand from his pocket to rub at the back of his neck as he stared down at the floor.

"Look—"

"She won't even talk to me," Van interrupted, slicing his eyes over to Grant. He shrugged, rolling his shoulders. "Won't respond to texts. Wouldn't let me see her. Just... pushed me away last night. Made me let her go and watch her walk away crying." He raised his eyes to Grant's. "Do you know what it feels like to have to witness your own heart breaking while it beats inside someone else's chest? To watch that part of your heart walk away, knowing how badly she's hurting? I get that none of this makes any fucking sense, man. People don't meet the way we met her. Don't have this... this connection right off the bat. They don't fall in love with strangers they met in a hotel bar. But I did. And so did she. Somehow, she loved us both... and now she's pushing me away because you made her believe you hate her, when you love her, too."

He watched as Grant swallowed hard, his dark gaze dropping once again to the floor between his feet.

"You better figure out how to make this right. Because if we lose her because you're a giant dickhead..."

Grant nodded, still looking at the floor. They had never talked about Hope, how that weekend had changed them, about their feelings. How finding her again had changed them. He took another drink of the bourbon. Maybe it was the liquor combined with the incomprehensible heartache he was suffering that had finally loosened his tongue. Whatever it was, he couldn't stop the words from falling out of him. He'd bottled them up since Chicago, respecting Grant's wishes to not speak about it, sweeping everything under the rug like their generation had been taught, as if that made everything disappear.

"We don't even know that this is something that we can make work, Van..."

"We spent every goddamn waking second with her for an

entire weekend. And I realize that's not enough time to really get to know someone... but I know everything I need to. I know that she's kind, and beautiful, and so willing to put her fragile heart in our unworthy hands. I know that she's scared. That she's never felt like this before, either. That we both feel it in our gut—" he said, thumping his fist against his abdomen and staring up at the ceiling, "—that if we could just figure it out... this thing could be magic. Isn't that what soulmates are, anyway? Magic living in separate bodies?"

"Van... you're drunk." Grant sighed, rubbing his hand over the back of his neck again. He knew he was drunk and making no sense. But it made sense to *him*. They were magic, all three of them, but only when they were together. He just needed Grant to see it, too. "We don't share like this, for a reason."

"Because we get jealous."

Grant nodded, raising his eyes to his. "Yes," he answered gruffly. "This is going to get messy."

Van shrugged, taking another drink of the bourbon. It was almost empty now. "I'd rather have messy with her than without."

Grant shook his head and sighed again. "How are we supposed to make this work, huh? We what? Flip a coin for who gets to sleep with her at night? Draw straws to see whose bed she sleeps in? Rock-paper-scissors for who gets to cuddle with her on the couch? I mean, are we supposed to—you know, us together—?"

"I don't know, Grant," Van muttered, shrugging his shoulders again. "I don't have any of those answers. But I know I want to at least fucking try to make this work with her. We've been best friends for years. We already fucking live together. We get along, for the most part, other than this! I love you, man. That's not to say I want your dick in my ass, but if that's what you need—"

"Jesus, Van," Grant huffed, backing away from the door and rolling his shoulders. He grunted a snort of a laugh. Van watched as Grant strode over to the edge of the bed and stared, shocked, as Grant bent down and kissed him. It was mostly chaste, as Van was too shocked to respond, and when Grant pulled away, they stared at each other. "Feel anything?"

"No," Van said, which was the truth. Not revulsion, but no spark, either. Grant nodded.

"Me either. I love you, too, buddy, but not like that. Okay?" Grant muttered, straightening. Grant plucked the bourbon out of his hand and downed the rest of it before handing the empty glass back to Van. He backed away toward the door again, leaning against the doorframe once more. "I know I—fuck, I love sharing her with you. I love it. I won't lie and say I don't get off on watching her with you. Knowing we both make her come, watching her take both of us... It's fucking hot. But I don't know how to share her every single day, Van. This is an entirely different dynamic than a hot as fuck one night stand. I need my space, so the three of us sleeping in one fucking bed isn't gonna work. But having to split our time with her... that doesn't work either. In Chicago, it was just some fucking pipe dream, fun and exciting to think about. Finding that one person that makes your soul feel like it's on fire... but knowing that I have to share that fire with you, too? In reality, in the here and now, it's fucking terrifying. What if I can't make her as happy as you can, huh? What if she never feels the same for me as she does for you, and over time she just... stops coming to me? I couldn't handle that. Having her here, but knowing I'm not what she wants..."

"So you self-sabotage us both?" Van asked, swinging his legs over the side of the bed and standing. He swayed slightly, though he wasn't sure if it was from the alcohol or lack of sleep. Probably both. "I don't see Hope being like that, Grant. She's crazy about you. She wants both of us, not just one or the other. She won't settle for one or the other because she won't choose. Can't we just figure it out, all three of us? Because we're kind of doing her an injustice by assuming all of this without even talking to her. If she'll ever talk to us again. You need to apologize. Soon, before she tries to run."

"Do you think she will?" Grant asked, and Van nodded solemnly.

"I think she's scared and hurt enough to want to, yeah," Van said quietly.

"Where can I find her?" Grant asked, raising his eyes to Van's.

"Thought you'd never ask." He told him her sister's address, and Grant entered it into his phone's GPS, not that he would need it. It was simple enough to find. "Bring her home to both of us, okay?"

Chapter Nineteen

T he rain behind him was fitting. Cold and dreary and it sank into his bones while the steady patter of raindrops on the sidewalk behind him and on the small covered porch over him dulled everything else around him. It was somber and gloomy and matched the feeling in his gut. He knocked on the door, and then a moment later he could see a shadow as she passed by the window on the right side of the door. It opened just a few inches and her mouth opened in surprise when she saw him standing on the tiny concrete landing. He watched as her gaze fell on the bruise blooming beneath his left eye.

"What are you doing here?" she asked, her voice quiet and husky. The puffiness around her blue eyes and the redness at the tip of her nose was testament to the crying she'd done, and it ate at him mercilessly. She clutched at the edge of the door with her fingers, half hiding behind it. What looked like an extra-long t-shirt covered her from neck to mid-thigh, her legs bare beneath it. A long, thin sweater type thing covered her arms and hung at her sides, revealing the slope of one breast that wasn't concealed by the door she was using as a shield. She shifted from one bare foot to the other and he realized she was afraid of him. Fuck.

"Van told me where to find you," he said quietly. It was reminiscent of her words from the day prior.

She scoffed, rolling her eyes as she snapped, "Van can mind his own business though, right?" He watched as tears filled her eyes and she blinked rapidly, quickly dropping her gaze from his. "Please go away, Grant. I don't... I don't want to see you."

"Did I hurt you?" he asked quickly, throwing a hand out to brace against the door as she made to close it. She swallowed hard and he saw her grip on the edge of the door tighten until her knuckles were white. He could see the red marks still etched into her wrists from her panties being wrapped around them. "Yesterday. Did I...did I hurt you?"

"Probably not in the way you think," she whispered, keeping her eyes down. "What do you care, anyway?"

"*Hope*," he pleaded quietly, refusing to let her close the door. "Let me make it better. Please. I have no excuse for my behavior. I was... I don't deserve a second chance, I know that. Please, butterfly."

"*Don't... don't call me that*," she gritted out, her lips pulling into a thin line. The pain in her voice... it made his chest tighten in agony. "You don't get to call me that anymore."

"Hope, please—"

"*Caterpillar*," she whispered, her voice breaking on the word, and he watched as her lower lip wobbled precariously. A tear slid down her cheek, followed quickly by another, and he froze.

She was safe wording him. His chest caved in and the realization of just how much damage his actions in the office had done truly sank in.

"Please, Grant. Leave me alone," she begged, raising her eyes to his finally. The tears that rimmed her eyes gutted him. Her next words stilled his heart. Van had been right. "I can't—I can't do this, Grant. Whatever that was... I can't do it again. I'll be leaving as soon as I can figure out where I'm going next. I already said good-bye to Van... I told you I couldn't choose, and

I won't. And I won't make you two choose, either. You two are best friends, it should stay that way. I'm sorry I ruined everything—"

"Stop it," he ground out, his voice low and ragged. She stuttered to a stop and more tears slid down her cheeks as she stared up at him. He softened his voice, pleading gently, "You didn't ruin anything, Hope. *I* ruined this. *I'm* the one to blame, not you. I fucked everything up because *I* was a coward, baby girl." She didn't fight when he gently pushed the door open further and didn't stop him when he cupped her face in his hands. She looked so tiny in comparison to his size, so fragile and precious. His thumbs slid over her cheeks, swiping the tears away as her lower lip wobbled. Her breathing was erratic through slightly parted lips, and he knew she was moments away from crying in earnest. "I am so sorry, Hope," he whispered, leaning close so that he could look directly into her eyes as he spoke. "I was unfairly cruel and I don't deserve your forgiveness, baby girl. I know I don't. I will get on my knees and grovel every day for the rest of my days if that's what it takes to convince you to stay."

"Grant." He was so close now he could feel her breath on his lips as she whimpered so softly it cut him to his core. "Don't... don't hurt me. Please. I couldn't survive it..."

"Oh, Hope. I'm sorry. I promise I will never hurt you, never again," he whispered brokenly. It killed him. He'd hurt her deeply, and it was going to take a lot of work to get her to trust him again. "Let me make it right, baby girl."

He used his foot to close the door behind him, and then he kissed her. Softly. Sweetly. Like he should have the first moment he'd seen her in the restaurant. Pouring all the tenderness he could muster into the kiss, he gathered her into his arms gently until she was as close to him as he could get her. He sighed when he felt her arms wrap around his waist, her fingers fisting in the fabric of the shirt at his sides as she kissed him back. Fuck, she tasted so good. Like blueberries and honey. He pressed sipping kisses to her lips, over her cheeks, her temples, down her neck. She arched into his touch, and he growled in appreciation.

"There's my baby girl," he murmured huskily when she pressed her body against his fully, arching into him. He stroked his hand down her hair, over her back. "My beautiful butterfly."

Gathering her into his arms, he lifted her, making her squeak in surprise. He walked them to the couch, where he sat down, settling her in his lap. Her legs bracketed his hips, her shins resting on the cushions on either side of his hips. His hands slid from the underside of her bottom over the round curves and her breath caught, and he watched as pain passed across her face briefly.

"Fuck, baby girl," he breathed, shaking his head sadly. He smoothed his palms over the swell of her bottom gently. "I did hurt you."

She swallowed hard and lowered her gaze from his. She whispered, "It's just tender, is all…"

Sliding his hands up her back to her shoulders, he brushed her blonde hair away from her face as he shook his head again. "God I'm sorry, Hope," he murmured miserably. Tucking her hair behind her ears, he let his fingers drift down the long strands over her shoulders. "I'm sorry. Please let me fix this, butterfly."

"Grant, just kiss me," she pleaded on a whisper, and so he did. He kissed her deeply, slowly. Fuck he'd missed kissing her. She was perfect, so in tune to him, and to Van. It was like she'd been made for him, for them. For both of them. Together.

They kissed and kissed, softly, sweetly. Over and over again. He was rock hard in his jeans, but he did nothing but kiss her. When she finally pulled away, breathless, she tucked herself against his chest and buried her face in his neck.

"You don't get to punish me like that anymore," she whispered against the skin of his throat, tucking herself into him, her body relaxing against his. "Not when you're angry."

Guilt gnawed at his gut. He smoothed his hands down her hair, over the softness of her back, and back up again, making sure to avoid the tender curves of her butt. He rested his cheek against her temple, moving his lips in her hair. "I can't apologize to you enough for what happened in my office, Hope. I have no excuse for how I acted. I broke every one of my rules in that room, baby girl, and I don't deserve your forgiveness. In my head, we had talked about it, in Chicago...and I rationalized it by getting your consent beforehand. But not like that, and I knew it. I took it too far. I was cruel and betrayed your trust in that situation. I don't blame you for not trusting me not to hurt you again, butterfly. And I'm so sorry."

Her arms were tucked between their chests, her head resting on his shoulder, and he could feel her lips as they moved against his neck. The junction of her thighs was still pressed against his lap, her thighs straddling his hips, but neither of them moved. He cradled her against him, simply holding her. Needing her against him.

"I was scared," she whispered then, and his heart ached. He tightened his arms around her. "In Chicago. I had never felt the way I did with you two, had never dreamed that anything like what happened with us could be real. I panicked. I told myself it was all in my head, that there was no way that you would feel the same way I did. Convinced myself it was just one crazy, incredible weekend. And I ran." He felt her back expand under his arms with her shuddering breath, then the soft exhalation she made against his throat. Snuggling in deeper into his arms, she continued, "I hated myself as soon as the door closed. I already wanted to turn around and bang on the door, pray that one of you would wake up and let me back in... I cried all the way out, Grant. I knew then that my entire life was changed, and it terrified me. We agreed no personal details. No last names. No hometowns. No phone numbers. I mean, how is this ever supposed to work in the real world? People don't... society doesn't like things that aren't normal. This isn't normal, and it's a small town and—"

"Shhh," he said gently, lifting her chin with his fingers until she looked at him. Fuck she was so beautiful. He'd missed her. So fucking much. "I know we agreed. Which is why I was so damn angry. I knew I shouldn't have agreed to that, and I did anyway. Because I knew that first night, Hope."

"Knew what?" she asked, searching his eyes with her own.

He reached up and tucked her hair behind her ear, before cupping her cheek in his hand. "That I had found what I'd been looking for my entire life, without even realizing it. You made me whole again, baby girl, for the first time in a very long time. And when I realized you'd left... it broke something inside of me. Something I hadn't thought was even capable of breaking."

"I don't know how to do any of this, Grant," she murmured. "This whole thing terrifies me. How can I feel what I feel for you... and for Van, at the same time? Every construct of relationships that I've ever known, everything we're taught... is that it's not supposed to be like this. That I have to choose one or the other. And I can't. I didn't want to that night. I can't now. But now Van is mad at me, too... And no one is going to understand—*how is something like this ever supposed to work*—"

Clasping her face between his hands, he leaned forward and kissed her, shushing her panicked monologue with his mouth. "Van is not mad at you, baby girl. He's mad at me, but I can handle him. We will figure it out. All of us. We said that night that you're ours, and we meant it. This is new for Van and I as well. We've shared—" She tensed at the words, and he smiled against her lips, "—don't get jealous, Hope. That was in the past. You're our present. And I think I can speak for both of us that we'd like you to be our future, too. We've never been romantically involved with anyone together. It will be something we need to work at and figure out."

"You would want that?" she asked, her delicately arched eyebrows raising in surprise.

He laughed lightly, smoothing his hands over her hair, brushing his fingers across her cheeks. "Do you think Van is going to let you walk away, baby girl? Do you think I could let you walk away again? I know that it's unconventional, and we will struggle with it, especially at first. I'm willing to try. I can't imagine going back to before. The last two months have been hell, Hope."

"It was for me, too," she murmured sadly, kissing him again. His heart thudded in his chest. "I missed you. I missed you both. I don't want to go back to before, either."

The door handle rattled and a moment later the door swung open as he glanced over. A fluffy, white muzzled golden retriever padded over the threshold, shaking raindrops from its thick fur. A half a heartbeat later, a woman entered, wearing a bright teal raincoat with the hood pulled up over her head, and a pair of red Hunter muck boots covered her feet. Pushing the hood off her head, he recognized one of his usual Friday night ladies, the curvy woman with strawberry blonde hair, the same one that had been at the table with Hope when he'd first seen her. Jade, he thought he remembered.

"Uhh—" Hope mumbled from where she was, still draped over his lap and chest. The other woman's head whipped over toward them.

"Oh!" she gasped, her gaze bouncing from his to Hope's and back again. Recognition dawned in her eyes and the look she gave him was decidedly chilly. "Umm. Hey."

Hope pushed herself away from his chest, though she still straddled his lap, her bare thighs bracketing his. "Uhh. Jade, this is Grant." Jade nodded once in acknowledgment, but didn't move other than to cross her arms over her chest. The fluffy, though still damp, golden retriever padded over to them, resting his white muzzle on the couch cushion next to Hope's leg. "Grant, this is my sister, Jade. And this is Bruno."

"We've met," Jade muttered, one strawberry blonde brow rising as she stared at him. Turning her gaze back to her sister, she asked, "I take it he apologized? Profusely?"

"Adequate groveling took place," Hope teased softly, laying

one hand against his chest. He covered her hand with his, his thumb strumming along the back of her hand.

Notching one hip out, she pursed her lips and narrowed her eyes on him. "I'm going to warn you right now, Mr. Price; I don't care how much of a hotshot you are in this town, if you *ever* make my sister cry like you did...we're going to have problems. Capiche?"

"Understood, Jade," he said softly, nodding. He liked her, even if it was going to take a while for her to like him, too. He would grovel for her sister's approval, if needed.

Jade pursed her lips once more and then sighed, turning away and heading into the kitchen, giving them a modicum of privacy. Grant strummed his fingers along the back of Hope's hand again, drawing her attention back to him. "I promised a very upset and quite drunk Van that I would bring you home to both of us. What do you say, baby girl? Come home with me? Please?"

When she didn't answer right away, he smiled gently and brought her fingers to his lips, kissing them softly.

"It's okay, you don't have to say yes," he said quietly, keeping his voice low. Jade flounced around the kitchen nosily, on purpose, he assumed. He caught her stealing furtive glances over at them when she didn't think he was watching and one corner of his mouth quirked up slightly. "If you're not ready, I understand. Just know that Van and I very much would like to see you, baby girl."

She nodded, flexing her fingers and trailing her fingertips across his lips, over his thick beard. She brushed her fingers gently over the bruise beneath his eye. "I think I'd like to go with you," she said softly. "If that's okay."

He smiled and nodded. "That's more than okay, baby girl." He patted her hip gently, careful to avoid the curves of her ass, and suggested, "Why don't you go get a bag together, and then I'll take you home to Van."

"You'll stay with us though, right?" she asked, cupping his jaw in her hand, those blue eyes searching his. "You won't leave?"

"I'll stay," he whispered, turning his head to press his lips to the palm of her hand. She nodded, and he smiled against her palm. "I missed you, Hope. My heart hasn't been the same since you left it in Chicago."

"I left part of mine in that hotel room, too," she murmured quietly. He leaned forward and captured her lips with his, not caring that her sister was still in the next room, probably shamelessly spying. When they parted, she whispered, "Take me home, Grant."

Chapter Twenty

Grant pulled into the garage, parking next to Van's sleek Lexus, and then caught her hand. "Don't touch that door," he told her, and she smiled, nodding. He exited the vehicle, rounding it to come and open her door, reaching a hand down to assist her out. He then took her bag, the same black backpack that Van had sent her home with, repacked with her toiletries and a change of clothes. He slung it over his shoulder, and it looked tiny in comparison to his size, making her giggle. He squeezed her hand in his as he led her to the door.

Pushing it open, he let her enter before him. She had made it down the hall and just entered the living room when Van rounded the corner and spotted her. She smiled over at him and he rushed forward, wrapping his arms fully around her waist and hauling her against him. His mouth crashed down on hers, frantic, matching her own need. His arms were banded around her so tightly, it was as if he was trying to imprint her on his body. Not that she minded one bit.

"Don't you ever do that to me again," he murmured against her lips before kissing her again thoroughly. They kissed and kissed, her hands fisting into his blonde locks. "You're ours, remember that, little one."

She nodded, brushing her lips against his. "Yours." Then, leaning back in Van's arms, she turned and reached one hand out to Grant, who was standing several feet away, leaning against the wall, watching them. He hesitated for a moment before stepping forward, taking her hand in his. She pulled him closer and looked up at him. "And yours."

"Ours, baby girl," Grant murmured with a gentle smile that tugged at every heartstring in her soul.

"I want you," she murmured, still staring at Grant, then turned to look at Van. "I don't want to wait anymore. Please."

Van grinned down at her, and her heartbeat tripled in her chest. He was just so unfairly handsome. He leaned down, running his lips along her jaw and down her neck, then whispered darkly, "Do you like being shared, little one?"

"Fuck yes," she whispered back, arching her throat to give him better access. She felt Grant's fingers slide around her throat, twisting her head so that he could cover her mouth with his in a languid, deep kiss that turned her knees to jelly. He pressed against her back and she ground her ass against his lap, moaning into his mouth when she felt him growing hard against her.

Grant nipped her lower lip with his teeth and she sighed into his mouth. He chuckled and placed his hands firmly on the heavy slope of her waist. "As much as I want to, baby girl, I think I need to sit this one out."

"What—no—" she whimpered, reaching for his mouth with hers again. "Grant..."

He ducked his head and pressed his lips to the curve of her neck, where her shoulder met her nape. "I want to watch, butterfly. I already got to have you all to myself... and I didn't do it right. I want to watch Van take care of you."

"But..."

"We will play, after," he whispered huskily. "And I'll be right here. I just want to watch."

"But, Grant—"

Grant shushed her words with his mouth again, and he nodded, just slightly. "I punished you for something you didn't do. This is *my* punishment for not taking care of you the way I should have. For not listening to you, when all you wanted was to wait for both of us. I need to watch you come apart properly, baby girl, before I can be part of it. This is my penance, and my way of apologizing to both of you."

Grant backed away from her and Van gripped her face in his hands, turning her to look at him. Tears stung her nose. "Van."

"Let's give him something worth watching, little one," he said, his voice low and husky as he ducked his head to kiss her. She matched his kiss, their tongues tangling wildly. "Drive him crazy from wanting you."

He released her face, grabbing her hand in his and pulling her down the hallway to his bedroom. She turned her head, just to make sure Grant was following. When they reached Van's room, Grant crossed the bedroom and sank into a chair that was stationed in the corner. Hope pouted at having him so far away, but he just gave her a lopsided grin, his white teeth showing up against the dark of his beard, and he nodded slowly.

Turning back to Van, she watched as he reached up with one hand and tugged the t-shirt up and over his head with one fluid motion, dropping it to the floor. He wore sweatpants, sharply tented by the erection straining beneath the fabric. She ached to put her hands on his body, run her fingers along the sharp edges and flat plains of his abs, up and over the defined pecs, smooth her palms over the muscles that curved and bunched along his shoulders, covered in tattoos.

He stepped forward, cupping her jaw in his hands again. "I'm going to worship every fucking inch of your body, Hope. I'm going to take my time as if I have the rest of my life to do so. I'm going to make you come, over and over again, so be prepared; because I won't stop, even when you beg."

"Ohmygod," she whispered, clamping her teeth over her bottom lip. His hands smoothed down her neck to the folds of her long sweater, pushing the material down her arms. She hadn't changed before Grant had tucked her into his car to bring her here. She blushed furiously, realizing she was wearing what could only be described as a muumuu. The long t-shirt material tunic was a pretty dusty blue color, but altogether unflattering in fit, though it did leave a large portion of her legs and thighs bare. When the duster cardigan had drifted to the floor from her fingertips, Van reached for the fabric at her thighs and pulled it up, revealing first the tops of her thick thighs, then her boy short style panties. Up it drifted, until the softness of her belly was exposed, then the under-curves of her breasts. When he pulled it over her head, it too fell to the floor in a heap.

A lacy, racerback style bralette was all that kept her breasts from being bare and she was thankful she'd changed out of her ugly sports bra before Grant had shown up at her sister's house. Her hair fell over her shoulders and down her back as she stared up at Van.

The backs of his knuckles dragged over the swell of each breast above the lace edge of her bralette. "You are so fucking beautiful," he whispered reverently, his green eyes covering every inch of her with an appreciative, hot gaze. Taking her hand in his, he brought her hand to the bulge tenting his sweatpants, and he groaned when her fingers wrapped around him. "You make me so fucking hard, Hope."

She exalted under his praise, the filthy, needy words filling her with bravado. She was acutely aware of Grant behind her, could feel his stare on her from where he sat across the room. She wondered if he, too, liked what he saw.

Van hooked his thumbs into the waistband of his sweats and tugged them down, along with his boxer briefs, stepping out of them when they pooled at his feet. Her mouth fell open and she wrapped her fingers around his impressive length, the steely hardness jumping under her touch. A bead of precum leaked from the broad head and she rotated the pad of her thumb over it, making him groan. He pumped his hips slowly, sliding his length through her hand and she watched, ridiculously turned on by it.

He tugged the lacy bralette up and over her head, freeing her breasts, and then his hands were on them, cupping them, squeezing gently, his fingers plucking at her already beaded nipples. She arched her back on a moan, pushing them into his hands and he chuckled, even as her fingers tightened around his length.

With one smooth motion, he slid his hands down her back and into the backside of her panties, pushing them down her thick thighs. Glancing over her shoulder at Grant, she blushed when she saw him, reclined back slightly in the chair, his slacks opened, cock out and in his hand, stroking it slowly. But then his gaze drifted down, and she saw pain and self-loathing flicker across his handsome features, and knew he was seeing the marks left on her from the night before.

"It doesn't hurt," she whispered to him, attempting to ease some of the guilt she could see on his face, in those beautiful dark eyes. "Grant..."

His eyes came back to hers. His hand had stilled. Van pressed a kiss to the tip of her shoulder. "Go to him," he whispered in her ear.

Stepping toward Grant, she braced her hands on the arms of the chair on either side of him, leaning forward and pressing her mouth to his. "I promise I'm okay," she said, breathing against his lips. "I like to be spanked, remember?"

"Not like that," he mumbled, though he pecked her lips with his gently, sweetly. "Never again, butterfly. I swear to you, I won't ever... I can't ever do that again. You're too precious to me, baby girl."

She kissed him, moving to wrap her fingers around his that

were slack around his hardness. Stroking him using both of their hands, she hummed appreciatively when he groaned, thrusting into their hands slowly. His other hand came up and cupped one heavy breast, teasing her nipple with his fingers. She breathed out a moan. "Are you going to touch yourself while you watch, big guy?"

A dark, wicked chuckle rumbled out of his chest. "I'm going to try not to come too fast already, butterfly. Now get back to Van and let him fuck you while I watch."

Feeling naughty, she stepped back just enough to be able to duck her head, taking the head of his cock into her mouth. She delighted in the shocked gasp that escaped him, felt his fingers sink into her hair, gathering it away from her face so he could watch as her lips wrapped around him.

"Oh fuck," he groaned through clenched teeth, thrusting up once, twice, but then lifted her off of him, pinning her chin between his fingers and raising her face so she was looking up at him through hooded eyes. "You're not behaving, baby girl. Don't make me break my promise and spank you."

She smiled mischievously and he growled menacingly at her. Then he raised his eyes over her shoulder and grinned darkly.

"Fuck, Hope. Look how hard Van is watching you suck my cock."

She straightened and turned. Van had sunk down onto the edge of the bed while he waited, but his hand was wrapped around his own cock, stroking languidly. "Did you like that?" she whispered, stepping toward him between his parted thighs and wrapping her arms around his neck loosely.

"Fuck yes," he mumbled, wrapping his arms around her waist, securing her to his front. "I will never get tired of watching you. What pleases you pleases me, little one." He kissed her then, spiraling his tongue into her mouth. They kissed until she was breathless and wet and aching. When he finally relinquished her mouth, she moaned breathily. "Now, are you going to let me worship this body?"

Nodding, she pushed her fingers up through his blonde hair, stroking it back away from his forehead. "Yes, Van."

"Good girl," he murmured huskily, grinning up at her. "I want you to lay down on your back and spread those legs for me."

She did as he instructed, lowering her body onto the mattress on her back, but then he grabbed her ankles and repositioned her so that Grant would have a better view, and she felt a flush of heat travel down her body. Van settled between her thighs, pushing them apart and up so that he could wrap his arms around the thickest part of them. He smoothed one palm over the butt cheek that had the darkest mark on it and she bit her lower lip at the slight tenderness, despite his gentle touch.

"I know they're tender... I'll bet you took these so well, though, didn't you, little one?" Van asked, pressing a kiss to the inside of her thigh even as his hands squeezed just below the bruises. "How wet did it make her, Grant?"

"So fucking wet," he answered from where he sat, and she turned her head to watch him. His chin rested in his fingers, elbow propped on one of the armrests, his other hand still stroking his cock, and his dark eyes were laser focused on her. His eyes softened then, as he murmured, "She did so good, but I didn't let her come. Make her come for us, Van."

Grant's huskily murmured praise and tortured admission turned her heart to fluttering frantically in her chest. Her fingers slid up through Van's hair as he continued to pepper kisses along the soft, jiggly insides of each of her thighs. She felt Van hum against her flesh and then his breath misted over her clit and she let her eyes sink closed just as his tongue flicked across that aching bud, once, twice. Her legs twitched where they were draped over his muscled arms and he chuckled darkly before settling in for his meal.

Her head rolled against the mattress beneath her as his tongue flicked, suckled, and teased her mercilessly, before sinking into her tightness. His arms tightened around her thighs, holding her firmly against his mouth. He hummed in appreciation when he felt her inner muscles begin clenching, and she held her breath as she came hard on his tongue, her body bowing off the bed with a sharp cry. Her feet pressed flat against the mattress, pressing her pussy against his mouth as spasms rocked through her.

"Fuck that's so hot," Grant grunted from across the room, and she opened her eyes, watching him as he stroked himself. Sometime during Van fucking her with his tongue, he had stripped his shirt off, because he sat bare chested, his pants lowered around his hips. It was sexy and wanton and so fucking hot watching him watch her, watching her and Van together. "Do it again, butterfly. Come on his face."

Van raised his head, grinned at her, then returned to what he was doing between her thighs, this time sinking first one, then two fingers inside her.

"Oh my god," she moaned, fisting her fingers in the sheet beneath her as his fingers found that spot deep inside, flicking it repeatedly. "Fuck. Oh Van, yes..."

"That's a good girl," Grant murmured, and she rolled her head to look at him again. Van's lips closed around her clit at the same time that his fingers went deep. She bit her lip sharply to keep the moan building in her throat from escaping. Van pinched the inside of her thigh with the hand that was still wrapped around one thigh and she gasped, tearing her eyes away from Grant and to him, where he was staring at her from between her thighs. "He wants to hear you, baby girl. Don't hold back. Let him know how good it feels."

Van nodded, telling her without words that Grant was correct and she whispered breathlessly, "Oh my god. I'm never going to recover from the two of you, will I?"

Grant chuckled and Van hummed against her pussy, thrusting his fingers and drawing her closer to another mind-numbing orgasm. Her body started to shake and then she was falling over that edge again, exploding around Van's fingers and against his tongue wildly.

While she continued to tremble from the force of her orgasm, Van crawled up her body, dropping kisses along every inch of her skin as he did so. When he reached her lips, he kissed her, sinking his tongue into her mouth and she blushed at tasting herself on his tongue.

And then he was gone, sitting back on his knees between her parted legs as he ran his hands over her body, every soft inch. His cock was hard between them and she reached for him, but he batted her hands away and smiled when she pouted. "This is about you, little one. We will play more later, but this is all you."

He stretched over to the side, reaching into the bedside table, and procuring a condom that he swiftly tore open and rolled onto his length before kneeling between her thighs again. He lifted her hips, settling them against the tops of his thighs, so that her hips were off the mattress completely. His hands spanned her waist, fingers and thumbs digging into the soft flesh there.

"Van, please," she whispered, writhing against him, trying to wriggle closer. He released one handhold on her hip, reaching down and guiding himself to her entrance, where he rubbed, drenching himself with the wetness there. And then she felt the pressure as the broad head of his cock pressed against her opening. His hand returned to her other hip, both hands tightening in hold as he sank in, slowly, inch by inch. His thumb found her clit, circling it as he pressed in, going as deep as he could, rocking his hips in slow, shallow thrusts. Her hands found his forearms, holding tight as they both moaned together. *God it felt so good*.

With the strength of his arms and thighs, he bounced her hips against his, the angle driving him in so deep her toes curled. Throwing one arm over her head, she fisted the sheet in her fingers as he rocked into her, again and again, slow and deep and oh so good. His thumb continued to stroke and circle her clit until she was a writhing, panting mess. She was going to come again. Her chest heaved, her breasts bouncing with every thrust, her cries becoming louder, longer, and more needy.

"Fuck yes," Van panted from above her, his eyes sweeping over her hotly. His body was taut, strained, the muscles of his arms bunching thickly as he bounced her on his length. "Come on, little one. Come for me. You do it so good."

"Yes, please—" she moaned low, her body spiraling into a free fall, and then she was coming, her inner walls convulsing around him as he pressed deep, and she sobbed with the intensity of it. "Ohhh, Van. Please. *Grant*—"

"I'm here, butterfly," he grunted from her left. He was still in the chair, his fist pumping hard and then she watched as he came too, ropes of cum painting his abs and chest as he let out a guttural groan. "You come so pretty, baby girl."

She trembled beneath Van, coming down from the high, and then Grant stood and picked up his discarded shirt off the floor, using it to wipe the mess he'd made on himself. She stared dazedly up at him as he stepped closer, bending low to kiss her hard and she arched upward into the kiss, his fingers sinking into her hair. And then he nodded to Van as he whispered, "I'll be here when you're done, butterfly. Let him take care of you."

Tears stung her nose again, realizing that Grant was giving her and Van time for just the two of them, and then he walked out of the bedroom, closing the door behind him. Van lowered himself over her, sliding his arms beneath her body and holding the back of her neck and shoulders in his hands. Her fingers scrabbled at his waist, pulling him closer, and then this mouth was on hers, fiercely, hungrily. He never slowed the pumping of his hips, continuing to slide in and out of her, deeply, slowly.

"I love you," Van panted as he broke the kiss, breathing the words against her mouth reverently. His fingers smoothed over her hair, bracketing her head on either side. They were as close as they could get, their hearts beating as one, pressed so close together. "I love you so much, Hope. I know it's crazy. But I do. You don't have to say it back—"

She sobbed brokenly, cupping his face with her hands as he continued to rock them together. "I love you, too." Tears slid down her cheeks and into her hair and he sipped at them sweetly. "I love you, Van."

"Fuck, little one," he groaned, pressing his forehead to hers as his hips picked up pace, thrusting harder, deeper. Half delirious, her mouth fell open in a soundless chant of *yes yes yes*, writhing beneath him as another orgasm barreled toward her. "Mine."

She nodded frantically, staring into those emerald green-depths as she shattered. "*Yours. Oh god*—"

"Yes, fuck, Hope," he groaned roughly, his hips hammering into hers, before they stuttered. "Christ, you fucking come so hard—"

"*Van!*" she cried sharply, coming harder than before, tucking her face into his neck to stifle the soul snatching scream that broke free of her throat. Her entire body convulsed, coming hard around him. He hammered into her once, twice more, then stilled as he came with a muffled shout, and she panted as she felt every pulse deep inside her.

He rolled them until she lay on top of him after removing the condom and tossing it aside. She rested her head on his chest, listening to the heavy cadence of his heart beneath her ear. His hands trailed up and down her nakedness, making her shiver, and she felt his smile against her temple where his mouth was pressed.

"I'm going to squash you," she mumbled tiredly, twisting her head to press her lips against his chest in idle kisses.

His arms tightened around her, running his palms over every inch that he could reach. "Feels perfect to me."

Propping her chin on his chest, she looked at him, her fingers sweeping lightly over his chest and shoulders. "I still can't believe any of this is real. Part of me is waiting to wake up and find out that I haven't actually found you... that this is all just a dream."

"If it is a dream, then I hope we never wake up," he said softly, tucking her hair behind her ear, his green eyes searching hers adoringly. God she loved him. So much. "I'll live in this dream with you forever."

"This is crazy, right?" she whispered, staring at him in wonder. "This is all so much so fast..."

"Is it, though?" he asked, pulling the sheet up over them both. She shifted, straddling his hips with her legs on the mattress and pushing herself up slightly, so that she was balanced on her elbows on either side of him. "Because to me it feels like it's always meant to be like this. We were meant to find you in Chicago. You were meant to be in our restaurant two nights ago." He smoothed his hands over her hair, playing with it down her back, the act so innocent and intimate. "I don't believe that we would have found you twice if it wasn't meant to be just like this, Hope."

"No one is going to understand..."

"So fuck 'em," he said glibly, and she rolled her eyes. "Hope, who cares? Who gives a rat's ass what anyone else outside of this house is going to think about us? It's a lifestyle that a lot of people have embraced all over the world. I don't care what anyone says. It's you and me and that grumpy fucker out there, and everyone else can take a hike."

Hope laughed, despite the anxiety that clawed at her. She kissed him, sweetly, slowly, before drawing away. "How do we make this work?"

"That is a discussion we need to have with all three of us. Preferably clothed, because I can't concentrate when you're naked."

"Why me?" she asked quietly. "I highly doubt I'm your usual type, Van..."

His hands smoothed down over the curves of her ass and down the backs of her thighs. "Why us? Grant and I are polar opposites from each other. One of us is bound to be more 'your type' than the other. So, why both of us?"

She pursed her lips and narrowed her eyes at him. "Touché."

He squeezed the backs of her thighs in his hands. "I need you to get up, because if we lay here like this for much longer, I'm going to get hard again and then I won't want to get out of this bed and let you go to Grant."

She laughed and sat up straighter. He groaned, his gaze zeroing in on her breasts, his hands coming up to cup them fully, his thumbs sweeping over her nipples. She breathed out a sigh, her head tipping back as each stroke of his thumbs shot sparks down into her core.

"Stop it," he groaned, sitting up as if hinged at the waist, releasing her breasts and bracketing her face in his hands. "Fuck you're gorgeous, and I don't want to stop. But that jealous beast out there is probably driving himself crazy waiting for us. Now get, woman."

She sighed against his lips and smiled, murmuring a quiet, "Yes, Chef."

He nipped her lower lip with his teeth, making her gasp. "You. Are. Trouble," he ground out, kissing her between words. She laughed throatily, but then swung her leg over to the side and climbed off the bed. He stood, too, and she stared at his nakedness, his impressive length that was again half hard. He swatted her lightly on the butt, below the light bruises, and then crossed the room to the dresser, pulling out two pairs of sweatpants and two t-shirts. He handed her a set and then pulled his own on. "Come on, love. Let's go find Grant."

Chapter Twenty-One

S tepping out of the hallway and into the living room, hand in hand with Van, Hope found Grant immediately. Standing in the kitchen on the other side of the marble topped island, he had changed clothes. He too, wore a pair of gray sweatpants and a long-sleeved t-shirt with the sleeves pushed up his forearms. Two pizza boxes and a fresh tossed salad sat on the counter, plates and silverware at the ready.

"You were busy," Van said with a chuckle, indicating the food as they entered the kitchen. Grant shrugged his impossibly wide shoulders as he glanced their direction. "Smells good."

"It sounded good, and I needed something to do while I waited," Grant said and then turned toward them. Hope released Van's hand and stepped forward, wrapping her arms around Grant's thick waist. His arms closed around her and she sighed when he rested his cheek on the top of her head. They remained that way for a long minute, and then she pulled back just enough to look up at him. He lowered his head and kissed her gently, so sweetly it made her heart ache in her chest. "Are you well?"

"I'm perfect," she whispered, smiling up at him, then turned her head and rested her cheek against his chest, listening to his heart beat steadily. Her stomach growled and he chuckled, the sound rumbling out of his chest and into her ear where it was pressed. She liked the sound of it. "Apparently I'm starving, though."

Grant pulled back and stepped over to the counter, lifting one of the pizza box lids. "It's no Chicago deep dish, but I think it'll do."

"Is that a Northmen?" Hope asked, her mouthwatering at the sight of the local favorite. She clapped her hands together and bounced where she stood. "Ugh I haven't had one of those in years."

"I thought it was a safe choice," he laughed, the sound low and gentle. This was the Grant she knew. The one she had fallen head over heels for in Chicago. Her gentle giant. He dished up two slices, put a helping of salad on her plate, and then handed it to her, which she took with a heartfelt thank you as her stomach growled again noisily. Van and Grant stepped up to the counter to dish their own plates, both men taking twice as much food as she had.

Van directed her to one of the plush bar stools pulled up to the opposite side of the island counter and she took a seat. Van snagged three beers out of the refrigerator and then he and Grant took seats to either side of her. She smiled at each of them in turn, happier than she'd been in a long time.

It felt like Chicago all over again. The companionability. The conversation. The laughter. The sexual tension and the sparks and heated glances that grew hotter as the time wore on.

She told them about applying for and securing the position at the school for early childhood development. "I love kids. I used to nanny for families in the area when I was a teen, and then through college. I feel like I've been waiting my entire life for my sister to give me a niece or nephew... not that that's going to happen anytime soon," she laughed.

Hope was surprised to learn that Van was the youngest of four, his siblings all significantly older than him. He had just turned thirty-six. "I was an oopsie," he laughed, taking a long drink of his second beer. They'd pushed their plates away, content and full. "My siblings were all in high school when my parents had me. They're both gone, but my older brother Noah and one of my sisters lives up here. My other sister is out in California."

She squeezed Van's hand. "I'm sorry to hear about your parents. I wish I could have met them."

He brought her fingers to his lips and kissed the knuckles gently. "They would have adored you."

She learned that Grant was forty-two and had a twin sister that was younger than him by two minutes and thirty-eight seconds. She was married and had two high school aged kids, though they lived downstate now. His parents were in the area, but elderly, and he'd set them up comfortably in a home not too far from himself, with live-in assistance.

They had migrated to the giant U-shaped sectional that took up most of the living room. Grant reclined in one corner, and she lay with her head in his lap, his fingers idly sifting through her hair, fanning it out over his abdomen and thighs. Her feet were in Van's lap, his legs stretched out next to her. She kept one hand on his leg, just to remain in contact. He squeezed one foot and she smiled over at him. The rain had never let up, remaining steady as the evening wore on. The sky out the wide windows was dark, the rain continuing to splatter against the panes in a soothing cadence.

"Jenny, our hostess, reminds me of my niece. They lived up here for a long time, but my sister's husband got a job offer he couldn't refuse downstate, so they headed south. I try to get down to see them once every few months," he said, sweeping her hair off her shoulder, just to start strumming through it again. It felt so good. "Especially after..."

She felt him tense and looked up at him. Was this the big thing? Whatever it was that Van had alluded to, that he had said was Grant's story to tell? Clasping his hand in hers, she tucked his arm against her chest and kissed his fingers.

She saw his gaze drift to Van and she glanced over just in time to see Van nod slowly. Grant took a deep breath in, letting it out in a heavy exhale. His hand cupped her jaw from beneath her chin, his fingers sweeping over the underside of her jaw, beneath her ear. "Ten years ago, I was diagnosed with cancer. Prostate." Her mouth fell open slightly, shocked, and her heart rate tripled in her chest. He smiled down at her. "We caught it early, started treatment, and within three years I was in remission and have some incredibly lucky stars to thank that it remains that way." Brushing his other hand up through his hair and then smoothing it over his beard, he continued on a chuckle, "The chemo made my hair fall out, and when it came back, it came back a whole lot grayer than I expected."

Hope shifted so that she could sit up, swiveling to look at Van and then scooting closer to Grant. "But you're okay now, right?"

He threaded his fingers through her hair and nodded. "Yes, butterfly, I'm okay now. I still get anxious at my yearly checkups."

"That's understandable," she said, reaching up and smoothing her hand over his heavily silver threaded hair.

Grant turned her face up to his and said solemnly, "Hope. I need you to know something, and I understand if it changes your mind about me... about us."

She swallowed hard, but nodded slowly. "Okay."

"I was married, once, back when I was sick. When I went through chemo and radiation... because of the kind of cancer and the treatment, we were told... Hope, baby girl." He sighed heavily, his mouth turning down at the corners. Jealousy crashed through her at the thought of someone else having his heart. "If you stay... are kids something you see in your future?"

Understanding dawned, the green tinge of jealousy fading slightly, and she smoothed her hand over his cheek. "I have always hoped so."

"I may never be able to give that to you," he admitted quietly, his dark eyes sad as he stared at her. She smiled, tears pricking her nose.

"It's not a deal breaker, Grant," she whispered earnestly, shaking her head.

"It was once... so I just need to know," he said softly, sadly.

"Your wife?" she asked, her brows drawing closer as the tears pricked her eyes. He nodded, brushing her hair away from her face. She shook her head. "I just want you. And we can practice, right? If we ever decide to try?"

He laughed then, his white teeth showing up against the darkness of his beard. "I'll practice putting a baby in you as often as you want, Hope."

She smiled, a blush tingeing her cheeks at the thought. She turned to Van, who was still reclining in his corner of the couch. "What about you? Are babies something you want in the future?"

"I hadn't ever given it much thought, to be honest," he said, reaching out a hand. She tucked hers in his and he squeezed lightly. "It's not like I've had any real prospects in the wings. Until you. If babies are what you want, I'll do my part to give them to you when we're ready, little one."

Tears stung her nose again and she smiled radiantly at Van, who smiled back, his green eyes crinkling at the corners. She looked back to Grant. "Is that something you'd be okay with?"

"If I can't give you babies, Hope, I would be ecstatic to watch you carry Van's," he said. "That wouldn't bother me. As long as it makes you happy."

Hope blew out a breath and blinked rapidly. "I feel like we're getting way ahead of ourselves," she laughed, glancing between them both. They laughed, too, and the heaviness that had settled over them dissipated.

"We have plenty of time to figure that out, if that's something you want. I would love to know if being here, with both of us, is what you want, Hope," Van said.

"As in, just for a while until you get tired of me?" she teased lightly, wrinkling her nose at him when he rolled his eyes.

"As if that is even a possibility," he muttered wryly, shaking his blonde head at her. "I can only speak for myself, but you already know how I feel about you, about us. All of us. This isn't some passing fling for me, Hope. This is my forever."

"Really?" she asked reverently, staring at him in wonder. He squeezed her hand again.

"Really. I could wax poetic about how I know in my soul that this is it for me. *You* are it for me. And if that means that you come with that big jealous brute over there—"

Grant launched a throw pillow at Van's head, and they all laughed as Van caught it. Hope turned to Grant, who was still stroking his fingers through her hair slowly. "Grant?" she asked.

He notched his head to the side and stared at Van for a long moment before turning those chocolate brown eyes on her. "He's right. I'm a jealous lover, Hope, I need you both to understand that. There will be times I will want you just for myself, and times that I want to share." He looked to Van. "If that's not something you're okay with, I need to know."

"I think we're both in agreement that there is a time and a place for both...and just one," he said, nodding. "There's a lot to figure out, but like I told you; I would rather try than go back to before."

"It could get messy," Grant rumbled, his voice deep and low, and Hope brought her eyes to his again. "This isn't going to be easy, and some days feelings are going to get hurt. Open communication and *honest communication* is going to be the key to making this work. For all three of us. No secrets. No lies. If something is upsetting you, either of you, we talk it out. Together."

"A strand of three cords is not easily unwoven..." Hope murmured, squeezing both of their hands. She smiled radiantly at first Van, then Grant. "I get to keep both of you."

Chapter Twenty-Two

"I'm not going to lie, all this talk about putting babies in you has made me horny as hell," Van said and grinned, leaning forward on the couch to grab her by the waist and haul her into his arms. "Anyone up for some practice?"

Hope laughed out loud, sinking into a long, languid kiss. Van's hands smoothed over her back, then slid beneath the t-shirt she was wearing, raising it up her back and then over her head.

"Oops," he breathed, grinning against her lips, his hands finding her now bare breasts. "What do you say, Grant? Think it's time our butterfly gets what she asked for?"

"What did you have in mind?" Grant rumbled from behind her, his voice deep and husky.

"I think our girl should get both of her men at the same time, don't you? That was her birthday wish, after all," he murmured against her mouth. Her breathing picked up its pace, knowing where he was taking this... "You like to be shared, right little one?" She nodded against his mouth, kissing him deeply. "Can you be a good girl for us and take us both?"

"Oh," she moaned throatily, nodding again. She knew exactly

where this was going... and she was ready. Nervous. But ready. "Yes. Please."

"Such a good girl asking for what you want," Grant murmured from where he sat. "But you know the rules, butterfly. We need to hear the words."

Oh fuck. She sat back on her heels, between them both. Grant's arm wrapped around her waist, his hand disappearing into the waistband of the sweatpants, his fingers finding her already wet and warm and aching for their touch. Van shifted forward, dropping his mouth to one of her nipples and sucking it greedily into his mouth, his hand flicking her other nipple nimbly, making her head toss back with a low moan as ribbons of desire coursed straight to her core. Her fingers sank into Van's hair, holding him against her and he hummed around her nipple. Grant's fingers delved deep, sinking into her. Her eyes closed and her thighs shook.

"Use your words, baby girl," Grant whispered huskily against her neck. "Tell us what you want."

"I want you," she mumbled brokenly, writhing against his hand and Van's magic mouth. "I want you both. At the same time. Both of you inside of me."

"Fuck you're such a good girl," Grant huffed out a groan. "You're going to take us so well, aren't you, Hope? You're going to open up and take both of our cocks inside this tight body."

"*Ohmygod*," she moaned, her breath hitching in her throat. She nodded, though a tingle of fear skittered over her. *Was she ready for this? For both of them?*

Van stood, pulling her up off the couch, and then Grant stood, wrapping her in his arms and kissing her deeply, hungrily. She melted into his body, humming in delight when she felt him, hard and heavy, against her middle. She heard the rustle of clothing from behind her, and when Grant finally ended their kiss, she looked over her shoulder to find a gloriously naked and rock-hard Van behind her. He reached for her and she went gladly, wrapping him in her arms as he dropped his mouth to hers. She felt hands at her hips, shoving the material of the sweatpants down her legs, and she stepped out of them when they reached her ankles, never surrendering from Van's kiss.

Kisses peppered her shoulders and down her spine to the curve of her ass. Grant's hands, so large and so gentle, smoothed over the marked flesh, dropping adoring kisses to each ample cheek before he stood once again. She turned in Van's arms, finding Grant as naked as she and Van. Reaching for Grant as tears stung her eyes, she kissed him tenderly. Her gentle giant. Her love.

"I love you," she breathed against his lips, her hands cupping either side of his face as he bent low to meet her kisses. "Grant."

His dark eyes misted slightly as he stared down at her, a small smile tilting up his lips beneath the beard she loved so much. "My butterfly," he whispered softly. "If you'll give me your forever, I'll spend every day of it loving you with everything I have in me."

She nodded against his mouth, tears sliding down her cheeks. "You have it, Grant. My forever is yours. As long as you want it."

He squeezed her close, kissing her soundly, before breaking the kiss and mumbling, "Van, get over here and get our girl ready."

Grant surprised her and picked her up then, his hands digging into the ample curves of her ass, and she gasped audibly. Her arms went around his neck instinctively, her legs wrapping around his wide hips.

"Grant!" she exclaimed, shocked. "Put me down—"

"I swear to God if you say one word about your weight or that you'll hurt me, butterfly, I will personally turn this pretty ass red, and not in the fun way. Fucking try me," Grant growled, hoisting her up so that her legs wrapped around his hips. She heard Van's retreating footsteps down the hallway toward his room, but he was back moments later. She shivered in anticipation.

Grant lifted her like she weighed nothing. Before she could allow herself to feel self-conscious about being lifted in a way that she admittedly never had been before, she felt Van against her back.

173

His mouth dropped to the meaty part of her shoulder, dragging his lips along her shoulder blade and up the curve of her neck. Fisting her hair in his fingers, he drew it aside and planted his mouth against the nape of her neck and she moaned. She loved them. *She loved them.*

"I'm going to take this ass," Van was murmuring against her neck, his hands gripping the underside of one thigh, the other trailing along her side, up toward her breast. He let the heaviness of her breast fill his palm at the same time that his fingers plucked at her nipple, and she shuddered. "I'm going to fill this pretty hole up with my cock while Grant takes this pussy. You're going to be so full of us, little one."

"Ohmygod," she breathed, reaching for Grant's mouth with her own. Van's hand at her thigh slid down and around the plumpness of her ass, sinking his fingers into her pussy, first one, then two. "No condoms. I want to feel you. I'm on birth control. I'm clean. Please, I just want to feel you."

"Fucking hell, you're so goddamn perfect," Van groaned. "Are you sure?"

"Yes. Please. There's no one else, never."

"Our girl is going to be so full of our cum it's going to drip out of her," Grant said, talking to Van even as his mouth continued to pepper hers with kisses. *Fuck, that was so hot.* He moved her so that his forearms were tucked beneath her knees, his hands gripping her thighs. Van worked his fingers in and out of her, over and over, until she was shaking in Grant's arms. Van's fingers thrummed against that special spot deep inside and she leaned forward, pressing her mouth to Grant's as she came with an explosion around Van's magic fingers. "Mmhmm. Get her ready for us."

When Van pulled his fingers from inside her, she mewled, going limp against Grant's chest. He was holding her as if she weighed nothing. The quiet pop of a bottle being clicked open roused her and she swallowed hard, staring into Grant's dark eyes. His fingers massaged the roundness of her hips as Van placed his fingers *there*, and she gasped at the coolness of the lube he was spreading over her tight hole. "We'll go slow, little one. Do you trust us?"

"Yes," she said, without hesitation. Her eyes never left Grant's as one of Van's fingers teased her tight opening before her body relaxed, letting him slide in. She moaned, clinging to Grant, even as her head fell back to rest against Van's chest. He worked her with one finger, then two, stretching her. When he added a third finger, she shuddered, her body tensing. "*Van.*"

"Relax, baby girl," Grant murmured, and she could feel it rumble through his wide chest and into hers where they were pressed together. "Let him in, Hope. Let him get you ready for us."

She nodded and looked up at Van behind her. He leaned down and kissed her deeply, languidly, continuing to move his fingers in her. "Oh, please, I want you."

"Who, baby girl?" Grant asked against the skin of her throat.

"Both of you. Always both of you, please," she sighed, her pussy clenching, desperate for something, too.

"I think she's ready," Van grunted from behind her and she nodded. He kissed her hard again. "Fuck I can't wait to fill you up. Lift her up a little, Grant."

She squeaked as Grant did as he asked, and then she felt the broad, blunt head of Van's cock against that part of her. She felt Van's mouth drop to the meaty part of her shoulder where it met her back as he pressed, heard his panting breaths as just the head of his cock slid inside. Her entire body wilted and he pressed open mouthed kisses to her shoulder as he slowly eased more of his hardness deeper. The fingers of one hand sifted through her hair gently, swiping it away from her face as he breathed reverently, "Fuck. That's a good girl. Let me in, little one. Just breathe. You're doing so good."

She bit her lower lip and closed her eyes. She was so full. Panting, she shifted in Grant's arms and she and Van moaned at the same time with the movement. He bottomed out and she whispered, "Oh my god. *Van*."

With Van seated fully inside her, he slid one arm beneath her hip on one side, his other hand drifting down and spreading wide on the curve of her ribs on the other as Grant shifted, loosening his hold just enough to release one arm. Both men had her weight balanced between them, as if she were as little as they claimed. Grant reached between them and took hold of his cock, positioning it at the entrance to her pussy. Opening her eyes, she stared into his. He rubbed the head of his cock against her wetness, slick from arousal and the lube Van had used, before pushing up.

"*Oh god*," she cried, her head falling back against Van's shoulder again. She was trembling, shaking between them, her body fighting against the intrusion of both of them inside her. It was too much. They were too big, there was no way they were both going to fit. They were going to break her, split her open, *ruin her*, she was sure of it.

"Oh, *baby girl*," Van whispered reverently against her temple, using Grant's nickname for her. He held onto her tighter, her shaking intensifying as Grant delved ever deeper. Stretching her beyond what she thought she could handle. She panted, writhing between them, fighting the ache that accompanied them both. Tears gathered at the corners of her eyes as she squeezed them shut. "You're doing so good. Stretching open to take both of our cocks like such a good girl. We've got you. You just open up and take us." His hips rolled against her ass, not quite enough to move inside her, but enough that she felt every inch of him as Grant pushed in, slowly, thick inch by thick inch. Her fingers scrabbled at Grant's bicep, her other hand grabbing a handhold on Van's forearm as they worked to fit them both inside her. The stretch was almost too much, the fullness so much more than she had expected, and still she trembled between them. She felt sweat dotting her forehead and a tear slid down her cheek, the pleasure and pain such a heady mixture it was nearly impossible to tell one from the other. "Are you okay, love?"

She nodded frantically, gasping breaths tearing from her throat as she shook her head. "*Oh god— it's too much—*"

"Just breathe, butterfly. You're doing so good, baby girl," Grant whispered, his voice thick and guttural, leaning forward to kiss away the tear that tracked down her cheek. "You're taking us both so well. So fucking *tight*. You're opening up so good for us. How does her ass feel, Van?"

"Fuck, so good. She's so tight," Van breathed from behind her, his mouth dropping to press against her shoulder. His fingers dug into her thigh where he was supporting her weight on one side. "Do you feel us, Hope? Do you feel how full you are of both of us? Is this how you wanted it to be? Not having to choose?"

"Yes!" she cried, her head tossing back and forth against his shoulder. Turning her head, she reached blindly for his mouth. She kissed him fiercely, their tongues tangling. Grant pushed the rest of the way in and she couldn't stop the mewling cry that escaped her when she felt him pulse inside her. She was so full. Van pressed his forehead to hers, panting raggedly against her mouth. "*I love you, I love you—*"

"You're ours," Van whispered, his lips moving against hers, and she smiled brilliantly against his lips, another tear tracking down her cheek. As one, they shifted, drawing out before working their way back in. She shuddered, the ache morphing slowly into pleasure. "*Ours.*"

"Yours," she breathed raggedly, more tears stinging her eyes. Turning, she reached for Grant's mouth with her own, kissing him deeply. "Yours. Yours."

"Fucking Christ," Van grunted, moving his hips in a steady rhythm, pulling out before sinking back in fully. "You're taking us so well. So perfect, Hope."

She let out a shuddering breath, pressing her hand flat against

Grant's chest, her back flush against Van's behind her. Shifting, she made a sound that was half moan, half whine.

"Use your words, butterfly. What do you need? Talk to us, Hope," Grant murmured, his voice low and gentle.

She was just so full, painfully, deliciously so. She was theirs. And they were hers. She loved them.

"Mine," she panted raggedly, hiccupping a soft sob. She kissed him again before turning to Van and capturing his mouth with hers, too. "You're mine, too. Both of you."

"That's our girl," Van whispered huskily against her mouth. They never stopped moving inside her, drawing her closer and closer to that precipice. She knew when she went over, she would never recover. But they would be there with her. Grant circled her jaw with his fingers, drawing her mouth from Van's and back to his. She delighted in the way they were both possessive of her in their own ways, and the way they shared her so well. She'd never felt more cherished than she did when she was with them.

Grant's hand drifted down and found her breast, his fingers plucking at her nipple while they continued kissing. The sensation rocketed straight through her to her core, causing her inner walls to clench tight, and she laughed breathlessly when both men groaned in unison. Their hips moved faster, sometimes sinking into her at the same time, going deep together, other times alternating, both sending her entire nervous system into a firework frenzy. Grant flicked her nipple again and she spasmed around them, and Van panted, "Fuck, if you keep doing that I'm not going to last."

Leaning back against Van's chest, she twisted her head and kissed him again, sobbing into his mouth when she felt Grant's mouth drop to her nipple, sucking it into his mouth and laving it with his nimble tongue. Her body spasmed around theirs, locked deep inside. She writhed in their arms when Grant's fingers found her clit, stroking it deftly with the pad of his thumb. She clenched around both of them again, making Van's hips stutter.

Van growled through clenched teeth, "Hope, I need you to stop that—"

"Don't you dare fucking stop—" Grant demanded, thrusting deep even as his tongue flicked her nipple again. Held between them, secure in their arms, she cried out and Grant hummed against her flesh as Van's fingers tightened where he held her.

"*Hope*—" Van groaned low, his breath catching in his throat. Half warning, half plea.

She was so close, her body already in free fall. Tossing her head wildly against Van's shoulder, she sobbed, "I can't stop, I'm going to—"

And then she detonated like a goddamn bomb, her entire body seizing with the force of her orgasm. Her toes curled. Her thighs shook. Her abs contracted. She came so hard that stars burst behind her tightly clenched eyelids. She might have stopped breathing, her heart hammering in her chest as her mouth dropped open in a silent scream.

Their hips hammered into hers, her orgasm pulling Van's from him with a low, guttural groan, his lips against her temple while her head was thrown back against his shoulder. His cock pulsed inside her ass, filling her, and then she sobbed, sucking in lungful after lungful of air when Grant followed moments later. There was nothing like this. Nothing would ever be like this. With them. Grant's forehead dropped to her shoulder as he growled through his orgasm, his hips making shallow, deep thrusts as he pumped her full of his cum. He wrapped both arms beneath her thighs again, spreading her wide around his hips. She was so full of them, and she never wanted it to end.

They remained as they were for long moments, panting into the semi darkness of the room. She was still held up by Grant's impossibly strong arms beneath her thighs and Van's hands gripping her waist. Grant raised his head, and she kissed him slowly, softly. So different from moments before and so fraught with emotion. Then Van's hand was at her throat when she pulled away from Grant, and he turned her face over her shoulder to his. They kissed and kissed. Long and slow and sweet. Nothing had ever felt so good. So right.

Her and Grant and Van.

She didn't want one without the other. If she ever had to choose between the two... no. She couldn't. It was impossible. The thought made her physically ill. She loved them. She loved them both and she knew it with every single fiber of her being. Had possibly loved them from the very beginning. There was no her without them. It was all together... or not at all. And that simply wasn't an option.

Grant slid out of her first, and then Van. She groaned, pinching her eyes shut in discomfort. As Grant lowered her to her feet, her legs trembled violently, her knees nearly buckling, and she was grateful for Van's hands still spanned across her waist. Together, they both held her as she regained her balance. Grant pressed his lips to her forehead and she leaned into his strength, though he too was shaking.

"Are you alright, love?" he asked, breathing unsteadily against her temple. Van's hands squeezed handfuls of her hips, then smoothed over them gently from behind. She nodded weakly, a soft, content smile tugging at her mouth. "Are you sure? Was it too painful—"

"It wasn't any more than what I could handle," she murmured, resting between them. "I'm okay, Grant. I promise."

"Aftercare is just as important as the sex, Hope," Grant said softly, smoothing his hands over her back. "Probably more so. Your body and your mind are going to come down from that high and without proper care afterward, the crash can be debilitating." His dark eyes grew sad then and he said quietly, "I didn't take care of you after... in my office. I pushed well past your limits and I knew it, and then left you as I did... Let me do it right this time."

"Oh," she whispered, staring up at him. He smoothed his hands down the backside of her arms and then lifted them so that her arms circled his neck. Bending slightly, he lifted her, one arm at her back and the other beneath her knees. "Grant—you don't need to carry me—"

"We're going to shower," Grant called over his shoulder to Van as he crossed the room to the stairs leading up to the second floor.

"That sounds like a good idea. I'll be here when you're done," Van said to them as Grant carried her up the stairs. She glanced over Grant's shoulder at Van, and he winked at her with a soft smile. She blew him a kiss a moment before he disappeared from sight.

Grant carried her down the upstairs hallway and stepped them into his bedroom. It was overtly masculine; dark wood furniture, polished wood floors, dark navy bedding on a king-sized bed and a TV hanging on the wall across from the bed. He didn't put her down, stepping through the tidy room to his own ensuite bathroom. He set her down, kissed her languidly, sweetly, and then stepped around her to the glass walled, walk in shower to turn the taps on to warm.

Within minutes the bathroom had begun to steam from the hot water in the shower, while Grant walked around gloriously, beautifully naked—which she fully delighted in—pulling towels down from a shelf and dug out extra toiletries. She recognized the shampoo and bodywash she liked to use and looked at him curiously. He shrugged his impossibly wide shoulders and looked sheepish.

"When you left Chicago... you left them in the bathroom in the hotel. I brought them with me, just so I could smell them when I missed you," he admitted quietly, his voice deep and low. Her heart melted and tears stung her nose again as he took her hand in his, drawing her with him into the shower. He slid the floor to ceiling glass door closed behind them, stepping them into the warm spray.

"Grant..." she whispered, stepping toward him. She smoothed her hands over his abdomen, hard beneath a layer of softness and up his chest, covered in crinkly, salt and pepper-streaked chest hair. His hands settled on the curve of her hips, his fingers digging into the flesh just above her bottom.

"We don't need to talk about Chicago," he murmured. "You're here now, and that's all that I need."

"I love you," she whispered, pouring every ounce of emotion she could muster into those three words. "Grant. I think I might have loved you the moment we met. Everything inside of me knew... everything was about to change."

"You gave my life meaning again, Hope," he said and then he chuckled lightly, one corner of his mouth turning up just the slightest. "You gave me hope for a future. Something I hadn't let myself truly think about in a decade, butterfly."

Chapter Twenty-Three

Wrapping her arms around his thick waist, she settled her cheek against his chest and closed her eyes, listening to the steady, rhythmic cadence of his heart as it beat beneath her ear. His arms folded around her, holding her close, and they remained that way for a long time, just reveling in the moment, in the closeness, the quiet. The steady thrum of the hot water as it rained down on them, over their shoulders and backs soothed some of the achiness in her limbs, dissipating the tightness that had begun to creep into her muscles.

Grant positioned them so that she could lean her head back under the spray of water to wet her hair fully, his fingers sliding through the wet strands. She watched him, his attention on his task, dark chocolate brown eyes focused on his hands in her hair. When all of her hair was thoroughly wetted, he reached around her and clicked open the top of the shampoo, squeezing it out into his palm, and then he methodically massaged it into her hair. Her eyes slid closed, leaning into his touch with a soft moan. It felt so good, his strong, capable fingers massaging the shampoo into her scalp, down the long strands. Her hands had returned to his waist, touching lightly, holding steadily as he worked. And then he tipped her chin up and kissed her lightly before rinsing her hair.

He did the same with the conditioner, sliding the cream through her hair and combing through with his fingers gently, working out any tangles, before rinsing it thoroughly. He was so gentle and thorough, dropping kisses to her forehead, her cheeks, her lips as he worked. If she wasn't already in love with him, she would have fallen hard and fast just from this alone, she mused dazedly.

Then he grabbed a washcloth, wetting it before squeezing out a dollop of her bodywash, and then placed it against her shoulders and washed every single inch of her. Over each shoulder, down each arm, over her chest—her nipples hardened and she sighed out a breathy moan when it dragged over them—down over her fleshy, soft stomach. He knelt on the shower floor, washing each thick thigh and down her calves. Bending her knee, he placed her foot on a low ledge, and then his hand and the washcloth were between her thighs and she blushed a thousand shades of red. He was gentle, adoring, as he took care of her where she ached the most. And when he turned her so that he could wash the backs of her thighs and over the curves of her bottom, he kissed the light bruises still marring her flesh. He stood, washing up her back. Her breathing was labored, short, panting breaths as his hands continued to move over her. She was wet and aching again.

Grant moved her forward so that she could step beneath the spray of water, rinsing her entire body of the bodywash, and then turned her to face him. They were so close she could feel him, hard and heavy, against her middle, but he ignored his erection as he continued to worship her. Because that's what it felt like he was doing.

They swapped spots then, and he rushed through washing his hair, scrubbed at his beard, then washed his body just as quickly before rinsing. Standing fully beneath the water to let it run over his head, face and body, Hope simply stared at him. His body was magnificent. So big and thick and hard and soft in all the right ways. His arms reached up to scrub at his hair to rinse the shampoo and the muscles in his massive arms bunched and shifted with each movement, making her mouth water. His abdomen contracted as he moved and she couldn't stop herself from lifting her hands and splaying them, palms flat, against them. His muscles jumped at the contact and she smiled. She ached to lower her hand and take hold of his hardness, but this was his show, and she didn't want to take away his glowing aftercare. She guessed he needed it just as much as she had.

When he was thoroughly clean and rinsed, he shut the water off and slid the glass door open, grabbing a towel and wrapping it around her before they stepped out. Grant hurriedly towel dried his upper body before slinging the second towel around his waist, tucking in the corner at his hip, and then reached for her again. Tears stung her eyes as he dried her off and then used a hairbrush to comb through her long hair. He dropped a kiss to the tip of her bare shoulder above the towel and she smiled up at him over her shoulder.

"Come on, we're not done yet," he murmured, taking her hand and leading her out of the bathroom to the bedroom. "Lay down on the bed, face down."

"Oh?" she asked, biting her lip and dropping her gaze to the bulge behind the towel. He chuckled, shaking his head.

"You're going to be sore," he said gently, turning her away from him and giving her a light shove toward the bed. "This isn't about sex right now, Hope."

She pouted, but nodded, making him chuckle again. She dropped the towel and climbed up onto the massive bed, shivering lightly from the sudden chill. She folded her hands beneath her head and rested her cheek on them, watching him as he moved around the room. He climbed onto the bed, straddling her thighs with his knees on the mattress on either side of her, a bottle of lotion in his hand. Uncapping it, he squeezed a generous portion into his palms and rubbed them together. The sound of the lotion sliding through his hands was strangely erotic and made her heart thud in her chest.

But then his hands were on her shoulders, and she couldn't stop the low, throaty moan that escaped her when his fingers squeezed and massaged the muscles there. He chuckled again, and she loved the sound of it.

His hands smoothed over her shoulders, her back, down the backside of her arms, over the mounds of her ass and backs of her thighs. She was a puddle, a warm, gooey, fully melted puddle when he finished. And so horny she ached.

"Grant, please..." she whispered, her cheek still resting on her stacked hands. She could feel him, full and heavy and hard against her bottom and she shifted, grinding up against him, delighting in the heavy groan that drifted to her. "Please."

"I don't want to hurt you," he whispered back, lowering his chest over her back, leaning over her braced on one hand beside her shoulder. The shift in position had pressed his lap more fully against her ass and she sighed wantonly, arching against him. He swore under his breath, tucking his nose into the groove of her neck and shoulder as he rocked against her. "*Hope.*"

"You won't," she whimpered, trying her best to spread her thighs, but they were pinned between his on either side of her. The hand not supporting his weight off her was running over her side, from hip all the way up to the side curve of one breast. "I need you. The way it should have been..."

"Fuck, baby girl," he groaned miserably, thrusting lightly against her. His mouth dragged over the nape of her neck, his beard tickling her spine. "We don't rush, understand? I'm going to take my time."

She nodded against her hands, whimpering, "Yes, Grant."

The hand at her waist disappeared and then she felt him nudging at the space between her thighs. "Shift your hips up just a little, yes, just like that." His whispered praise rang through her and made her light up from the inside. Her thighs parted just enough to allow him to press his fingers between them, finding her wet already. "Such a good girl. You tell me if this hurts, okay?"

She nodded, moaning when he sank his fingers in deep. She was tender, but it wasn't painful. "I'm okay, Grant. Please."

His fingers disappeared and then the broad, blunt head of his cock was at her entrance. Arching against him as he pushed in, she dropped her forehead to the mattress on a long moan. She was ready for him, and he sank all the way in, grinding his front against the backside of her thighs and ass. His forehead dropped to her shoulder, his mouth pressing hot, open-mouthed kisses to her spine as he rocked against her achingly slowly.

"I love you," he breathed against her skin, and she exalted in the passion charged words. His lips continued to pepper her skin with kisses, his beard tickling her. She arched against his slow thrusts. His chest was against her back, his weight braced on one forearm as it lay flat against the mattress beside her, his other hand constantly roving over every inch of her skin that he could reach. His tempo never increased, remaining a steady, slow, deep roll of his hips that took him out to the tip, then all the way back in, stealing her breath every time. "I love you, Hope."

"I love you," she whispered back over her shoulder. His lips pressed against her temple. Every roll of his hips sent him so deep, the tip of him grazing that spot deep inside.

"I want you to come for me," he whispered against her temple. "Can you do that, butterfly? I want to feel this pussy flutter for me."

"*Ohmygod*," she moaned brokenly, his pretty praise and filthy words causing an avalanche of mini explosions to erupt throughout her body. Her inner walls clenched around him, and he groaned fiercely in approval, his hips thrusting just a little harder, faster. She nodded, writhing beneath him. "Yes."

"You're going to give me three, Hope." His deep, low voice

rumbled through his chest and into her back. "One for each one I stole from you. I want number one. Give it to me, butterfly."

With his cock reaching as deep as he could go, hitting that special spot deep inside, she nodded frantically, her muscles tightening, heart threatening to pound its way out of her chest, and she fisted her fingers in the sheet beneath her. His mouth closed over the meaty part of her shoulder, taking a love bite sharp enough to make her cry out as she came around him, squeezing him deep. He grunted against her back, rocking his hips slowly, working her through the first orgasm and prolonging it. She shuddered and whimpered, sinking her teeth into the sheet as it rolled on and on.

"Fuck, that was a good girl," he panted, and she wished she could swivel her head enough to kiss him. His hand at her side squeezed tightly before soothing gently. "I fucking love how pretty you come, Hope."

Sucking lungful after lungful of air in, she moaned, rolling her hips against his as aftershocks coursed through her, squeezing him sporadically. He chuckled against her back before levering himself up on his hands, raising his chest off her back. Thrusting hard and deep, he pounded into her over and over again, the change in angle sending him deeper, harder than before. It wasn't long before she cried out sharply, on the edge of falling again. "Grant... oh fuck. I'm going to—"

"Two, butterfly," Grant growled from above her even as her body began to shake uncontrollably. "You're right there. Give me another one."

This one barreled through her swiftly, knocking the breath clear out of her lungs and she screamed silently, face pressed into the sheet as she came with an explosion around his hammering cock. He thrust hard, holding still, pressed fully against her as it coursed through her. He groaned roughly and she could feel him throbbing inside her.

"Fuck you're going to make me come," he growled on a laugh. Shifting and sliding out of her, he parted her thighs and lifted her hips into the air, notching her knees into the mattress, her torso pressed to the bed. He lined himself up and sank back into her, making slow, shallow thrusts. His hands smoothed over her ass and down her thighs, fingers trailing over her skin, making her shiver. "I'm never going to get enough of this, Hope, never going to get enough of you."

"I know," she whispered, turning her head to look at him over her shoulder. He was braced on his widespread knees, hands spanned across the small of her waist, resting against the wide slope of her hips. He was magnificent, and all hers. He continued making those slow, shallow thrusts, his hands never remaining still, always moving, touching everything he could.

"Hope," he groaned, throwing his head back as she squeezed her inner muscles around him. He shifted again, pulling out of her and laying on his back. Hauling her up and over him, she squeaked in surprise and settled her legs on either side of his hips. He wasted no time, guiding his cock back to her entrance and pulling her down sharply on top of him, sinking all the way in.

"Grant—"

"I want my third."

Fuck. Like this? she thought worriedly. Using her thighs, she lifted her body up and over his, then sank back down on him, his hands spreading wide along her ribcage. Her still damp hair clung to her shoulders and down her back. She braced her hands wide on his chest, palms flat, using them and her thighs as leverage as she moved over him. She bit her lip and stared down at him, fully aware that her entire soft, jiggly body was on full display for him.

Grabbing both of her hands in his, Grant tugged her forward until her chest rested against him, and then he released her hands, wrapping both of his arms around her so he could piston his hips upward, over and over again. She dropped her head to his shoulder and cried out, circling her hips against his, which only made her moan louder at the sensation. *So good.*

One of his hands found her throat, tilting her face up toward his. He kissed her, kissed her so deeply that tears burned her eyes. Pressing her forehead to his, she panted brokenly as he brought her to another soul snatching, earth shattering orgasm. Her body bowed, her thighs shaking violently as she came, sobbing with the intensity of it.

"Yes, fuck yes, Hope, just like that, *just like that*—" Grant growled raggedly, holding onto her tightly and using his hips to thrust hard upward again and again. He came with a guttural shout, and she felt him pulsing inside her, spilling into her with steady, hot bursts. Smoothing his hands over her hair, he peppered her forehead and temple with kisses as her body continued to shake. "Oh, good girl, that's my beautiful girl. You come so good, Hope."

Several tears tracked down her cheeks and he kissed them away tenderly, his hands still stroking her hair. This...this with Grant, was exactly what she'd needed. A reset. A reminder of just how incredible they were together. She loved him with every beat of her thundering heart.

Chapter Twenty-Four

Van showered and cleaned up the kitchen, putting away the leftover pizza and salad. When the unmistakable sound of Hope climaxing drifted down the stairs, he grinned, groaning lightly when his cock began to harden at the thought of what Grant was doing to their girl to elicit such a reaction from her.

He leaned against the counter, folding his arms across his chest. He knew that she and Grant had needed their time alone. Grant had punished himself thoroughly, beating himself up for the way he'd treated Hope in the office, though Van still didn't know the full details, and wasn't sure he wanted to know. It was in the past, and by the sound drifting down from Grant's bedroom, they were working things out just fine.

When they came down the stairs a short time later, Hope had her arm looped around Grant's waist, and he had one arm draped over her shoulders. Van watched as Grant dropped a kiss to her lips when she turned her face up to look at him, and the smile that graced her face turned Van's heart to putty. She was here, and she was glowing. This was where she was supposed to be.

She skipped over to him when she saw him, looping her arms

around his neck and kissing him soundly. His hands settled on her waist and they rocked together slowly.

"All better, little one?" he asked softly, and she nodded, resting her cheek on his chest with a contented sigh. "Good. Those sounded like good ones."

He delighted in the deep blush that tinged her cheeks as she peeked up at him through her blonde lashes. She was just so incredibly stunning; she took his breath away. Those blue eyes that he wanted to get lost in for the rest of his forever. Those full, pink lips that he could spend kissing for an eternity and never get enough of.

"I haven't come like this since Chicago," she whispered shyly.

"Well, I would fucking hope not," Grant mumbled from the refrigerator, where he'd plucked a bottled water and was chugging it. He pointed a finger at his own chest, then at Van and growled, "Your orgasms belong to us, butterfly. No one else."

"Yes, Grant," she murmured, smiling over at him as she tightened her arms around Van's waist. He grinned, dropping a kiss to the top of her head. Glancing up at him and then over to Grant, she asked softly, shyly, "I know this isn't Chicago and, Grant, I know you want your own space... but..."

Grant turned, setting the bottle of water down when she faltered. "What is it, baby girl?"

Van felt her swallow and she trembled lightly with nerves. He squeezed her gently, and she sighed, tightening her arms around him. "Please don't make me choose between you tonight. I don't want to sleep without either of you. Please."

Grant chuckled, picking the bottle of water back up and finishing it. "If you think either of us is going to let you sleep away from the other for a good while, you obviously don't know how this is going to work, baby girl."

Looking up at him and then over at Grant, he felt her body relax with relief and realized just how much that had been bothering her. "So, I don't have to choose?"

Van smiled, his heart trying its damndest to squeeze its way out of his chest. "That's the beauty, love. You made your wish. You never have to choose again, little one."

She smiled brilliantly, tucking herself back into him and reaching for Grant's hand, which she took and squeezed. "Good."

Chapter Twenty-Five

"I think I'm dehydrated," Van groaned, making Hope laugh. Grant chuckled from the other side of the bed, a book open in his lap. Hope lay between them in Van's wide bed, her fingers entwined with his free hand where they lay on his chest. Hope's back was pressed fully against Van's front, Van's arm draped around her. They were all naked, just the sheet pulled up to cover his lap and up to their naked torsos. This was quickly becoming his favorite; the lazy, quiet Sunday mornings together. They had settled into a routine with surprising ease.

Most nights they found their way into Van's bed, all three of them. But Grant had stolen Hope away a few times over the last several weeks, barricading them in his room and doing all the filthy, wonderful things to her body that he had dreamed about after Chicago.

Van would then reciprocate, stealing her away for a night, which he surprisingly didn't mind, because lord... the amount of sex they had was insane, and Grant fully understood Van's declaration of dehydration. She hadn't officially moved in, though she did stay with them every night. Maybe it was time to change that.

Her sister had slowly started to come around, though she still gave him that baleful glare from time to time. He was still working on winning her over. Grant had insisted on meeting her parents the week prior and the three of them had been honest about the nature of their relationship. Her parents had been surprisingly accepting of the relationship. Van had dazzled them with a delicious meal, but Grant hadn't missed the way her parents watched the way he and Van interacted with their daughter. This Hope, the one with the sleepy smile and shining blue eyes... with her shy blushes whenever he or Van would get caught staring... the way she danced when she ate without realizing she was even doing it... she was happy, content, and he knew that her parents could see it, too. He liked to think that he and Van were large in part of that.

"I've been thinking," Grant started slowly, closing his book and setting it aside. Hope's face fell in worry and he smiled over at her reassuringly. "I've been thinking it's kind of silly for you to keep bringing an overnight bag every day. All of your stuff is still at your sister's house, but you're here more often than not." When she stared up at him with wide eyes, he continued, "I know it's only been a few weeks, but what about this hasn't been a little unconventional?"

"Grant...?" she asked quietly, cautiously. He grinned again, squeezing her hand.

"Ready to make this official? Move in with us?" he asked, raising her hand to his mouth and pressing a kiss to her knuckles.

"You do know this is crazy, right?" she asked on a whisper, then turned to look at Van. "Are you sure about this? Both of you? You might not even like me that much."

Van laughed out loud, rolling his eyes and tucking her against his chest with his arm banded around her. "Right, we don't like you at all."

"Crazy or not, I haven't been anything but honest about how I feel," Grant said, and she turned her attention back to him. "And I want you here, butterfly. With us. So what do you say?"

The smile she sent his way was shy but radiant. "Okay. Yes."

She looked over to Van, who leaned down to kiss her. "If that's okay with you?"

"Little one, if he didn't ask you, I was going to," he murmured softly, glancing up at Grant. He nodded. He had figured as much. Grant didn't want to waste anymore time, and had trusted that Van didn't either.

"It's settled then," Grant said and stroked the back of her hand with his thumb. "You're stuck with us now, Hope."

"Stuck stay."

He laughed out loud. It made no sense, but the adoration in her tone and the love in those blue eyes sure made sense. "Stuck stay."

"How about our first official date, then? To celebrate?" Van asked from behind her.

"Like, out in public?" she asked, her blue eyes widening.

Van shrugged, his arm tightening around her waist. "I'm not ashamed of what we are. I don't think I'd like anything more than to shout it from the rooftops that you're ours."

"Okay," she said quietly, nodding. "No hiding."

Grant nodded, too, stroking the back of her hand with his thumb. "No hiding. You belong to us, and we belong to you."

Chapter Twenty-Six

"Well look what the cat dragged in," Jade muttered sourly from the couch, Bruno's head in her lap. Hope grimaced as she shut the front door. "Bruno, I think there's a stranger in our house."

"I'm *sooorrrry*," Hope mumbled, flopping into the empty corner of the couch and scratching Bruno's fluffy butt.

Jade sniffed disdainfully, but the dimple on her cheek from trying to suppress a smile was enough to tell Hope she'd already been forgiven. "The sex better be *fan-freaking-tastic*. You abandoned me for dick."

"But really, *really good* dick," Hope whispered, throwing her head back to rest on the back cushion of the couch with a sigh. "Like. Jade... I'm ruined for anyone else."

"Well, yeah, because you're getting it two at a time!" Jade laughed, throwing a throw pillow at her head. "I'd be fucking ruined, too!"

Hope wheezed with laughter and tucked the pillow into her lap, crossing her arms over it. An old habit of hiding her body that had never really gone away. Though Grant and Van more than made sure she knew how much they liked her body. Every inch of her.

"So just what brings you over here to my lowly apartment? Did you get amnesia and forget where you were living?" Jade asked with a smirk. She hauled herself up off the couch and padded into the kitchen, returning with their favorite two mismatched wine glasses and a bottle of Riesling, which she poured into the glasses and then handed one to Hope. "Poor Bruno thought you hated him."

Setting her wine down, she snuggled the old golden, smushing his white face between her hands as he licked her chin. "Oh, *Bruno*, I could never hate my best boy. Never ever ever."

"So, how are things, really?" Jade asked, settling back into her corner of the couch again. She sipped her wine and angled her body toward Hope, who did the same.

"Wonderful," Hope breathed, smiling. She shook her head and took a drink of her wine. "Jade, I can't even explain it. It's like... it's exactly how it was in Chicago. Only a million times better. God, they are so funny, Jade. So funny and kind and good lord, Van can cook. And Grant is so sweet, just like my giant teddy bear from that weekend..."

"No more grumpypants?" Jade asked seriously, pinning Hope with a levelling stare. "No more tears?"

"No more tears, no more mean grumpypants," Hope assured her earnestly. "He's quite good at groveling."

Jade harumphed cynically, eyeing her sister shrewdly over the top of her wine glass. "He better be. I meant it when I said if he ever makes you cry like that again—"

"I don't see that ever happening, Jade," Hope murmured with a smile. "It's like magic when we're together. I can't explain it. I knew it in Chicago and I ran because I was scared... I know you don't believe in all that soul mate mumbo jumbo, but..."

"When you know, you know, kind of thing?" Jade finished softly. Hope nodded.

"They feel like home," Hope whispered, running her finger around the edge of her wine glass. Tears pricked her eyes, but they were happy tears. "They feel like home to me, Jade."

Jade's eyes were suspiciously wet when Hope glanced up and she laughed sadly, dropping her eyes to her wine again. "You're leaving me, aren't you."

"Of course I'm not leaving you, you're my sister," Hope laughed, reaching out her hand to take Jade's.

"I just got you back. I thought we would have more time, the Mackenzie sisters back together and all," Jade murmured, shrugging.

"I'm literally just across town," Hope said softly, squeezing her sisters' hand. "And you're welcome to come over anytime, most nights they'll be gone at the restaurant and I'm home by myself—"

Jade squeezed her hand back and smiled at her. "You're moving in with them, though, huh. You called it home."

Hope sagged where she sat. "I did, didn't I?" Jade nodded, but smiled. "They asked me today. I don't have to—"

"If you think I'm going to stand between my sister and true love, you're crazy," she laughed, shaking her head. "You said it yourself; they're your home now. I can't be sad or unhappy for my little sister finding the kind of love most people spend their whole lives wishing for."

She was unsuccessful at stemming the tears that filled her eyes this time, and they slid down her cheeks. She swiped at them, laughing. "This is crazy, though, right? How insanely fast this all happened?"

"Is it?" Jade asked quietly, then wrinkled her nose and shook her head just slightly. "I don't believe that fate would bring people together like you three have if it wasn't meant for something big, Hope. You said it feels like magic; maybe it is?"

Hope nodded. Maybe it was. Soul mates, after all, were the best kind of magic.

Chapter Twenty-Seven

Stepping out of the bedroom and padding down the hallway, Hope stopped to take in the sight of the two men waiting for her. Grant wore a pair of dark jeans that fit his thick, muscular thighs. A buttery soft, navy-blue V-neck sweater covered his upper body and torso to perfection, the sleeves pushed to his forearms. His dark, silver-streaked hair and beard were trimmed and styled, and those dark, chocolate eyes roved over her with appreciation.

Van had chosen a pair of lighter wash jeans and paired it with a long sleeved, army green henley, the buttons left undone at his throat. His sleeves were pushed up his forearms as well, revealing the tattoos that decorated his arms down to his wrists. His blonde hair still looked damp and fell boyishly over his forehead. They were both so ridiculously handsome. And hers.

Jade had helped her carry several of her boxes to her car after finishing their wine, sending her off with a hug and a promise to come over for a girl's night later in the week. Grant and Van both helped her carry in her first boxes, officially moving her in, which had made Grant ecstatic. She dug through one box until she found an acceptable going out outfit, her favorite pair of black skinny jeans and a simple black long-sleeved shirt that hugged her ample curves. A soft, burnt orange colored scarf was draped around her neck, and she had styled her hair in loose waves down her back. Cognac brown, low-heeled booties covered her feet.

"Is it bad that I'm nervous?" she asked, crossing the living room toward them. "This is our first date... it sounds so silly, considering everything..."

Van grinned and tugged her into the circle of his arms as soon as she was close enough to reach. "You mean considering you've had both of our cocks in this beautiful body more times and in more ways than we can count?"

She laughed out loud, her nervousness abating. "You say the filthiest things..."

"But it made you laugh," he said softly, ducking his head to kiss her. "Fuck, now all I can think about is how fucking hot it was this morning when you—"

"I swear to god, if you talk about that right now, I'm going to get hard and then we'll never make it to dinner," Grant muttered, though he stepped up behind Hope, planting his hands on either side of her hips and gently thrusting his front against her ass. She laughed, wiggling against him. Both men groaned. "I'd like a replay of that tonight."

Making a quarter turn, she looped one arm around Grant's neck and pulled him down for a hot, open-mouthed kiss, the reminder of their morning sparking something deep in her belly.

Grant growled low in his throat, nipping her bottom lip sharply with his teeth. She gasped and then Grant circled her throat with his hand, squeezing just tight enough and pushing her away. The heat in his dark gaze turned her into a puddle. "Fucking dammit, butterfly, you naughty thing..."

"Let's go, before I strip these clothes off you and lay you out on this fucking countertop as my meal," Van grunted, slapping one ass cheek lightly. She laughed and pulled her arms from around both of them. Grant was rock hard in his jeans and she licked her lips with a grin. "Stop it, little one. I know that look, and we don't have time."

"Fine..." she whispered sulkily, pouting. Grant's hand returned to her throat, tipping her head up toward his. His breath misted over her face as he leaned close, and she whimpered softly.

"I want nothing more than to let you put my cock in your mouth and fuck this pretty throat, baby girl," he growled low, sending electricity zinging through her straight to her middle. "And if you behave, I'll let you suck me off while Van drives us home tonight."

"Holy shit," Hope moaned, nodding as much as his hand at her throat would allow.

"Jesus, now I'm fucking hard," Van groaned, palming his own dick through his jeans. Hope laughed throatily.

"Let's go," Grant growled, though a grin tugged at his lips.

"Yes, sir."

They managed to leave the condo and make it to their dinner reservation on time, though she was admittedly wet and aching by the time they arrived. Sitting in the backseat with Van while Grant drove, they had petted heavily through their clothes, kissing and teasing mercilessly. Hope had smiled angelically when both men had to adjust the erections they were both sporting.

The restaurant Van had chosen was an old favorite of hers, a family-owned Italian restaurant that had the best chicken parmigiana around. Grant requested a table instead of a booth, and they were led to one near the center of the room. Hope felt like they were on display... but she attributed it to nerves.

Grant held her chair for her, while Van spoke to the waiter that stopped at the table. He ordered a bottle of red wine and a basket of breadsticks, per Hope's request. As Grant gently pushed her chair in, she looked up at him and smiled. He bent low and pressed his mouth to hers in a quick, chaste kiss before taking his own seat. She blushed, glancing around, but no one seemed to be paying them any attention. She sat between them, the two of them facing each other across the small square table. Van took her hand in his and brought it to his lips, kissing her knuckles lightly.

"Just breathe," Van said softly, and she nodded. When the waiter returned with their wine and the basket of fresh, buttery breadsticks, she forgot her nerves because her mouth started watering. Van handed her one on a plate and she bit into it, closing her eyes in rapture, her body swaying in her seat. Van laughed lightly and said to Grant, "You're right. She does dance when she eats."

"I do not!" she protested, opening her eyes and staring at him, then Grant.

"You just were," Grant chuckled, reaching out to tuck a strand of hair behind her ear. He shook out his napkin and placed it in his lap before taking a breadstick for himself. "It's adorable, Hope. That's how we know you like something. You do a little happy dance."

She blushed again. "You're not supposed to pay that close attention," she whispered.

"We're not supposed to pay attention to what our girl likes?" Grant asked, leaning forward over the corner of the table. He pecked another kiss to her lips. "It's our job, baby girl. To take care of you."

Van handed Hope a small, leather-bound menu, and then passed one to Grant over the center of the table. "I haven't been here in ages."

"I'm sure you don't do a lot of eating out," Hope laughed.

"He's a terrible dinner guest," Grant grunted, glaring at Van over the top of his own menu. Van shrugged and didn't look the bit apologetic.

"I just know that I can usually make it better," he said simply. Hope rolled her eyes with a smile, but knew it to be true... his cooking was phenomenal. "But I do like their Bolognese here."

Hope sipped her wine, letting her gaze travel from Grant on her left, his big, husky and strong body so inviting, to Van on her right. His blonde hair fell over his brow again and she reached out, pushing it off his forehead. He caught her hand and kissed her palm, his green eyes searching hers intensely.

"I love you," she whispered quietly, cupping his cheek with her palm, before turning her gaze to Grant. "And you. I love you, too. Thank you for not making me choose."

"Never," Grant murmured low, his dark eyes soft as he stared into hers. "Thank you for having the courage to choose both of us."

Tears stung her nose and she blinked rapidly, but twin tears slid down her cheeks. "Ugh, you're going to make me cry. I'm going to ruin my makeup." Van chuckled, squeezing her hand. She took a shuddering breath in then placed her napkin on the table. "I'll be right back, I just want to make sure my mascara isn't making a mess of my face."

She stood, but Van didn't release her hand, pulling her toward him. She ducked to kiss him softly, sweetly, before weaving her way through the tables to the restroom.

She used the restroom, then stepped out to look in the mirror. Her mascara was a little smudged, but not terribly so. She used a paper towel to dab at the smudges as an older woman stepped into the restroom. Tossing the mascara blackened paper towel into the garbage, she washed her hands, and Hope smiled awkwardly to the older woman standing at the sink beside her. The woman was staring at her, a look of disgust on her face. Hope glanced in the mirror as if to check for a piece of food stuck in her teeth, then dropped her gaze to her feet to check for toilet paper on her shoe. Nothing. But still the woman stared.

Hope pulled another paper towel out of the dispenser and began drying her hands.

"You should be ashamed of yourself."

Hope froze, drawn up short and she turned to stare at the woman, her mouth hanging open slightly. She glanced around, as if to make sure the woman was indeed speaking to her, but they were the only two in the ladies restroom. She shook her head slowly, trying to make sense of what the woman was speaking of. She recognized the woman; she had been sitting at a table near them. "I'm sorry, what?"

The woman's lips thinned, and then her shoulders straightened as if drawing courage, and she whispered, "You're a slut."

"Excuse me?" Hope gasped, shock and outrage battling for supremacy. Tears stung her nose. She blinked rapidly. *What the fuck?* "I'm sorry...?"

"This is a public, family environment," the woman hissed. "There are... *there are children here*. You should be ashamed of yourself. Being with two men..."

Hope gasped, realizing what the woman must have seen, her interactions with both Van and Grant. Hope drew herself up straighter, refusing to let this woman intimidate her. "I don't think my life is of any concern to you, and if it's offensive to you, don't watch."

"You're doing it right out in the open!" the woman hissed, outraged. Her face was turning red and she was trembling. "We shouldn't be subjected to your whoring—"

A startled laugh choked out of her. Hope shook her head in astonishment and said quietly, "I'm sorry, we're done here."

"You think this is funny?" the woman screeched, furious now at Hope's apparent insolence. "What is going to happen to those people having to witness your loose morals—"

"Polyamory isn't contagious, I think you'll be fine," Hope snapped, angry now in her own right. She was shaking now, too.

"Your taboo lifestyle is—"

"Taboo lifestyle? What is so taboo about loving two people?" Hope gasped, losing her composure. The woman's face turned a mottled red in rage. "And who are you to judge me for who I've fallen in love with?"

The woman scoffed in disgust. "This isn't how society works. You choose. One or the other. Only those with no self-respect would demean themselves by allowing two men—" her words cut off suddenly and her face pulled into a look of utter disgust, as though she was too horrified to even finish the sentence.

Hope's head tipped back as though she'd been physically struck. *Wow.* "So I'm a slut for being in love with two incredible men—"

The laugh that escaped the woman this time was ugly, born of pure ignorance and hate, and made Hope's chest tighten as the woman hissed, "You can't possibly love them both—"

"Do you like sunsets?" she asked suddenly, cutting the woman off. She looked at her as if Hope had lost her mind. Maybe she had. She was shaking.

"Who doesn't love sunsets. What does this have to do with—"

"What about Christmas lights?" Hope asked, again interrupting. "Do you like those, too?"

The woman took a longer time to answer, her lips pulling tight. "Yes."

"Does your enjoyment of one negate or invalidate the enjoyment you get from the other?" Hope asked.

The woman looked like she was choking on her tongue. She swallowed. "No."

"Could you choose to never love one again, simply because you love the other?" Hope asked, pressing her point.

The woman stayed resolutely silent, trembling where she stood. Hope knew there was no point in trying to convince this stranger of her lifestyle, but she refused to walk away without explaining.

"My love for both of those men is not diminished in any capacity because of my love for the other. Grant...is like snuggling next to a wood fire, cozy Sunday mornings, reading in bed together. He is strength and warmth and kindness. And Van is sunshine on your face, and your favorite comfort food, rainy days watching a storm roll in on the front porch, and so much goodness..." Tears stung her nose and she tried to keep them from filling her eyes. She failed miserably, the tears sliding down her cheeks, and she shrugged, smiling. "Asking me to choose is not only impossible, but unfathomable to me. I would rather stop breathing than choose between them. I love them. It's as simple and finite as that. Nothing anyone is going to say to me is going to change that." She shrugged her shoulders and smiled again. "Most people consider themselves lucky if they can find one great love in their lives... How lucky am I that I found two at the same time?"

When the woman didn't respond, Hope nodded, then walked out of the restroom.

As she approached their table, Grant looked up with a smile, but it quickly fell as he took in her expression, the way she was trembling, the tears in her eyes. He stood, towering over her and demanded, "What's wrong?"

"Nothing," she whispered, placing her hand on his forearm. "Grant, it's nothing. Please, just sit down. I'm okay."

The older woman returned to her seat several tables away, her face pinched as though she smelled something disgusting, but she kept her gaze away from Hope and her two men.

"Please," she whispered, tugging him back into his seat. He sat reluctantly, his hand finding hers as he stared at her. She brought his hand to her mouth and kissed it gently. "I am on a date with the two loves of my life. Nothing can take that away from me."

Van's hand slid over her thigh under the table. "Did you hear that, Grant? We're the loves of her life."

She smiled over at him and nodded, then turned to look at Grant once more, tears gathering in her eyes again. "There are some love stories where two isn't enough... And I'm so glad that this is our story. I got my wish. I get both of you. For always."

"For always, butterfly," Grant agreed, his dark eyes shining. "Ours."

She looked over to Van and she let out a quiet sigh, another tear tracking down her cheek. He cupped her cheek gently, swiping the tear away, his own green eyes luminous with unshed tears. "Ours, little one."

She nodded, smiling radiantly, her heart fairly bursting from her chest, her love for both of them consuming her entirely. "Yours."

Epilogue

THREE YEARS LATER

Grant paced, hands shoved into his pockets.

Van swore, dragging his fingers up through his hair.

Hope bounced on the balls of her feet, her hands clasped tightly together under her chin. Her finger worried the twin wedding bands on either side of her engagement ring. Her heart was in her throat, her stomach in knots. She stared at the towel on the bathroom counter, then glanced at the clock on the wall.

Two minutes left.

Van stepped up beside her, dropping his chin to the top of her head, his arms curled around her shoulders, one hand trailing through her hair.

"Would you fucking stop pacing—" Van snapped at Grant, who only grunted in response, not slowing his pacing in the slightest.

Forty-five seconds. Hope was fairly vibrating with nervous energy. This was it. She knew it had to be it, finally. Finally.

Grant strode over toward them, clasping her face between his hands and forcing her face up to his. His mouth was nearly on hers, as he breathed, "If it's not—"

"If it's not, we'll keep trying," she whispered, closing her hands over his where they were clasped on either side of her face. She stroked the wide gold band that surrounded his left ring finger.

"If I can't—"

"If you can't, it won't make me love you any less," Hope whispered earnestly, reaching for his mouth with hers. Grant kissed her hard, and she could feel all the fear and tension in him. When he broke the kiss, he looked over to Van and said gruffly, "You—"

Van nodded, clasping Grant's shoulder with one hand and squeezing tightly. "It's all of us, no matter what. That hasn't changed, Grant."

Hope glanced at the clock. "I think it's safe to look, now. Oh my god, I'm scared."

Grant kissed her again, sending his tongue into her mouth and she moaned breathily. "Fuck I'm scared, too, baby girl."

Grant backed away, stepping to her side. She found his hand and squeezed it tightly, then reached for Van's with her other one as they stepped toward the towel on the counter, their wedding bands clinking as they clasped their fingers together tightly. Van reached for the towel, then looked down at her. "Are we ready?"

"Yes!" Hope cried, smiling and laughing and crying all at the same time, bouncing where she stood. Van lifted the towel, revealing the small plastic applicator that had been hiding beneath it. As one, they leaned closer to see it.

They had agreed that they would give it one year, one year of trying just her and Grant. Van could have bought stock in condoms, they'd used so many, giving Grant the best possible chance. They had five months of failed attempts.

Hope's eyes zeroed in on the two lines, which quickly turned to four as tears blurred her vision. Her entire body sagged, and Van slapped Grant on the back with a whoop as Grant whispered, "Holy shit. *Holy shit!*"

Hope's arms went around his neck at the same time that his arms circled her waist, hauling her clear off the floor as he hugged her, his mouth crashing down on hers. She cried, clasping him as close as she possibly could.

"God dammit, Hope, I fucking love you so much," she heard him rasp against her mouth. "Butterfly..." She nodded frantically against his mouth, smiling and laughing and crying, her hands cupping his bewhiskered cheeks in her palms, her fingers catching the tears that wetted his cheeks. He set her down and his large, strong hands spanned over her soft belly. "My baby is in here."

"Your baby is in here," she laughed, hiccupping, covering his hands with hers. Van spun her around and lifted her, wrapping her in his arms. They kissed, smiling against each other's mouths.

"Does this mean I can stop wearing condoms?" Van teased, and Hope laughed, nodding. "Thank fuck. I miss feeling you on my bare cock. If we hurry—"

A disgruntled wail erupted from the bedroom, and they laughed together before he released her, disappearing into the bedroom. Grant pulled her back into his arms, kissing her fiercely. Tears gathered in her eyes when her husband returned a moment later carrying their nine-month-old daughter Ava in his arm, her tiny face red from crying, her blonde curls tousled from her nap. Van bounced her in his arm against his chest, pressing a kiss to her chubby, tear-stained cheek.

"There she is, there's our Mama," Van crooned, stepping up close to her and Grant. Ava reached for Hope as soon as she was within arm's reach. "And there's Daddy Bear, too."

"Did Daddy come get you?" Hope asked, taking their daughter from Van's arms. Ava rested her cheek against Hope's shoulder with a tiny baby sigh, her little hand extending toward Grant, who tucked one finger into her little hand for her to hold. He ducked his head and pressed a kiss to the soft curls on the top of her head sweetly. "Daddy Bear's princess."

Grant tucked himself against Hope's back, resting his chin on the top of her head, and Van stepped to her side, covering Ava's back with a warm hand and rubbing gently. Hope raised her eyes to Van's and he leaned down, pressing a kiss to her mouth. Hope leaned back against Grant's chest, relishing the warmth of him against her, with Van's hand covering hers where it rested against Ava's little back. Standing between her husbands—the loves of her life—she sighed happily.

Her heart was so full it ached, in the best way possible, standing between the two men who held her heart and body and soul completely. There was no her without them. She loved them, with her whole being. For whatever forever they were gifted...

Because there were some love stories where two just wasn't enough... and this was hers.

With the best birthday wish to ever come true.

Coming November 2024 to the Holiday Novella Collection!

Meet Me Under the Mistletoe
featuring Noelle and Theo in a friends to lovers, unrequited love,
sweet and spicy Christmas novella!

Acknowledgments

I truly cannot believe that we are here at the end of my fifth book already, and the second in my newest series! What an adventure this has been, and I truly feel so blessed to be doing what I love! Thank you all for your continued love and support throughout this journey!

Mom, you were my first and always my biggest fan, and the best proofreader around. Without your love and support this wouldn't have been possible! You knew when I was fifteen that I would be here one day, even when I doubted it myself. On to book Six (holy crap!) already with so many others on the way! I love you!

Nick my love, thank you for letting me hide away at my desk for hours—and sometimes days—on end. Thank you for messaging me that my breakfast, lunch, or dinner was waiting for me when I was ready for it, because you knew I wouldn't even think about eating (thank you, Chef). Thank you for your unwavering support, faith, and enthusiasm for this passion of mine. Without you and the love you give me, I wouldn't have started writing again. Without your support, I wouldn't be able to do this full-time. You are my biggest cheerleader, my love. You are my forever Prince Charming. I love you!

Kara, you have been such a champion in my corner, for your unwavering faith in these stories and in me! And THANK YOU for excitedly and willingly volunteering as tribute to come with me to all our author events! I can't wait to see what kind of trouble we can get into!

Haley, KG, Ava, and Melanie; Thank you to these wonderful fellow authors that I have had the pleasure of being on this journey with! Haley, thank you for always being a critical and willing sounding board, and the Tessa to my Jodi! KG, Ava, Melanie, HOLY MOLY, I'm so glad I met you and feel fortunate to be traversing this new journey with you and a million thank you's for taking me under your wings! Thank you, ladies! I can't wait to see you all at future events!

Melody with Aurora Publicity, thank you sooo much for the absolutely gorgeous cover! KG, thank you for always being a willing mentor and for the STUNNING interior formatting!

To my **Booktok Baddies**, April and all the wonderful **Smut Sluts**, **The SmutHood**, and Courtney and Dorothy and all the **Michigan Booktok Babes**, THANK YOU for allowing me to be unapologetic in my shameless promotions and all of you that have recommended The *Petoskey Stone Series* and this *Holiday Romance Collection* to this absolutely voracious world of spicy romance readers! To my amazing **Street Team**, THANK YOU for loving these crazy characters and their stories as much as I do! I hope you all love these three as much as I do! I can't wait to bring back Noelle and Theo next in the *Holiday Novella Collection*, as well as Roxy and Travis in the next for the *Petoskey Stone Series*! I love all of you!

To all the people that are not named but have beta read, listened to me venting or joined in my excitement over each new milestone, and all those that have rooted for me in this scary and enthralling journey, thank you! I wouldn't be here without you!

Lastly, to all my readers, old and new, this has only been possible because of the love and support you've shown me and these characters. I hope you love reading their story as much as I've loved writing it. Hope, Van, and Grant's story literally just fell out of me and onto the page, and I'm so glad they're here in all their spicy glory! I look forward to introducing you to MANY more in the future! Thank you!

About the Author

Danielle Baker, romance author of the *Petoskey Stone Series*, including *Love Unbound*, *Best Kept Secrets*, and *A Heart So Wild*, and the *Holiday Romance Novella Collection*, including *Be Mine, Valentine* and *Birthday Wishes*, was born and raised in the beautiful city of Petoskey, nestled on the crystalline shores of Lake Michigan. She is married to the love of her life, Nicholas, and they have four children between them. Danielle's love of writing began while she was in high school. She wrote a slew of short stories and had written three novels by the time she graduated. Life got busy and writing was put on hold for many years while she started her family. At the urging of her mother, sister, and husband, Danielle was given the boost she needed to "get back in the saddle" and keep reaching for her lifelong dream of becoming a published author. When Danielle isn't working, writing, or spending time with her family, she can be found with a cup of coffee in one hand and a book in the other.

Also by Danielle Baker

PETOSKEY STONE SERIES

Love Unbound

Best Kept Secrets

A Heart So Wild

Holiday Romance Novella Collection

Be Mine, Valentine

Birthday Wishes

Upcoming Novels in the Petoskey Stone Series!

When Hearts Collide - coming summer 2024!

Stay With Me

Hard To Love

That One Night

Upcoming in the Holiday Romance Novella Collection!

Meet Me Under the Mistletoe

Lucky In Love

A Saturday in June

Halloween Night

Midnight Kiss

Keep watch for announcements for The Bliss Garden Girls Series and the STORM! Prequel Novella Trilogy in 2024/2025!

9 798988 045670